The War Mage Series

Homecoming

Jake Logan

Cover artwork © 2015 by Marc Ducrow

Cover design by Niki Lenhart
nikilen-designs.com

Published by Paper Angel Press
paperangelpress.com

ISBN 978-1-944412-20-3 (Trade Paperback)

10 9 8 7 6 5 4 3 2 1

FIRST EDITION

Dedication

*To Mom, who surrounded me with books
and gave me my first typewriter at 15.
I still miss you.*

Author's Note

I have not been to war. I have tried to empathize with what it feels like to come home after a long deployment. If I'm off, send me some comments; if I'm spot on, send me some comments. I'd love to hear from you at grimaulkin.com.

ONE

"How many fucking goats does this guy have?" Mark beeped the horn.

The platoon was stalled outside a small village three kilometers outside of Forward Operating Base Wilson in Kandahar, Afghanistan. A total of eight men waited for a shepherd, his charges, and his son or grandson herding the stragglers behind.

Mark laid on the horn again.

"He's not going to move any faster," said Sergeant Custer. His curly red hair, slightly too long for regulation, was tucked in a helmet.

"Makes me feel better, sir."

From the back came a voice, "The faster he moves, the longer we stay outside the wire." Brent Rogers, the one they

1

called Wizard, seemed to always have the right words to calm Mark down.

Mark leaned forward, his broad forehead resting on the steering wheel. Custer glanced behind him at the two men in the back seat of the Humvee. All of them had done this dozens of times before. All of them came home in one piece.

It was almost Ramadan, the high holy Islamic holiday when people fasted during the day and celebrated at night. Sometimes those celebrations involved fires, alcohol, and guns, which never mixed well even in the best of circumstances. As long as they got back before sunset, they were safe.

Finally the last few goats cleared the road. Mark stomped on the gas and they lurched forward in a cloud of dust.

"Left," said Brent. He said it in a normal voice, but Mark turned left immediately. The other Humvee behind them also jerked left.

Brent did not have a gun across his lap like the man next to him in the Humvee. He carried a natural wood staff with no decorations. He wore the usual uniform of the Army: desert camo tunic and pants, Kevlar body armor, steel helmet. His oval face showed some tenseness in the set of his jaw. Custer said to him, "Anything there?"

"A feeling," said Brent.

Custer nodded. The young blond kid to the left of Brent looked down at the stick, then at Brent, catching his large eyes. Cory gave a barely audible sigh and looked out the bullet-proof window. Brent said, "Sorry, Cory. Doing my job."

"It's freaky," said Cory. He was 19 and baby-faced; not like Brent, who, even though he was only four years older, had lost his baby-face and looked now like a chiseled veteran made of marble: an oval head set on a neck of ropes for tendons, with short brown hair, hazel eyes hidden by the wrap-around sunglasses that all the men wore. Brent's nose was classic northern European, with full, plump lips and an angular jaw.

"Be happy that he's saved our hide more than once with his 'freaky'," said the man in the gun turret above them.

The Humvee slowed down again. Kids played ball in the street between two buildings in a new village. As with the goat herder, they didn't seem in a hurry to move. Mark beeped the horn. Mark was much bigger than Brent. Mark was the ox of the team: tall, broad, a pro-wrestler's body. He didn't have the patience of an ox, however.

The kids finally completed whatever round they were on and Mark drove slowly between two groups of teenagers. The men all watched them warily, wondering which one of them might have a bomb. The kids kept all their gazes in turn.

"Will we make it?" said Custer. He turned back again to look at Brent.

Glancing out the window, Brent said, "This road is parallel to the one we were going to take. It might be even shorter."

"Good thing," said Mark, "Or I'd have to kick your ass, Wizard."

"Like the last time?"

"You cheated!"

"You said full contact."

"Full contact," Mark huffed, absently rubbing his broad chest. Cory made the sign of the cross. Brent caught the movement out of the corner of his eye but said nothing about it.

They hooked up eventually with an engineer platoon from the 3rd Infantry Division, who were cleaning up a street and shoring up a building that had been half-destroyed by mortar fire. The men all dismounted the vehicles. Mark got his rifle from the holster next to his seat. Cory got out, followed by Brent, who touched the ground with his staff before stepping out of the Humvee. He paused, getting a lay of the land and a sense of the air. Brent waved up at the men in the other vehicle, signaling an all-clear. The two machine gun turrets in both vehicles were manned.

The mission was expected to be generally easy. All they had to do was provide overwatch, making sure no one attacked the engineers. Some young kids came out of nowhere to watch the men work. Mark, although big and intimidating, had a soft spot for the boys. They liked the pens he brought with him.

Meanwhile, Custer and Jason, Custer's assistant from the other vehicle, talked up the locals in order to try and gather intelligence. The Taliban still held sway here, but Custer wanted to present the Americans as guides and assistants, not occupiers. Possibly the neighborhood might remember that the engineers were there to help, and not go over to the other side.

Brent patrolled the area like the rest of the men. Unlike many of the wizards in the Magic Corps, he was fit enough to carry his own pack. Other wizards stayed at the TOC — Tactical Operation Command, also known as the headquarters — and got soft. He worked best in the field.

He poked at the ground with the staff before reaching down to dig his fingers into the dirt. Mark asked, "Hey, whatcha doin', Wizard?"

"Listening for bombs," he said. He didn't find any IED's in the immediate vicinity. If he did, he'd blow them up himself from a distance by magic.

The engineers worked without incident, staving up what was left of a building, to make sure no one would get hurt going by it, and then they all mounted up. The engineers had three of their own trucks, so they led the convoy back to FOB Wilson.

Brent kept his eyes closed throughout the bumpy ride home, while the men watched warily around them. No one was on the street. Sundown was close.

Then the truck in front of them went up in the air with a ball of fire beneath it.

Mark slammed on the brakes, skidding to a stop while Brent's eyes flashed open. The truck that exploded bounced off of an invisible shield that was about a foot around the Humvee. The flying truck tipped over, landing on its side.

Cody ran out the side door, while Custer looked back at Brent. "Wizard…"

"I can't sense everything. I already told you, I can sense around me for fifteen feet, and that means this Humvee." Brent got out of the vehicle as other men rushed to the truck to pull out the driver and any passengers.

There were two wounded men, one screaming he was blind even as Cory wiped the blood from his eyes. The wounded man had a nasty gash across the top of his head which kept bleeding down.

The other wounded man had gotten out of the truck and stood holding his left arm close to his body. He saw the wand patch of the Magic Corps and the small red cross patch of a healer on Brent's uniform, and nodded calmly.

Brent closed his eyes again and held out his hands, as if in benediction. To him, the soldier before him was bathed in a gold aura with red splotches — the injuries.

The red splotches were in two major places: one at the soldier's left forearm and the other at his left shoulder. As Brent concentrated, the red light faded, flowing into the rest of the man's aura. The soldier gasped and moved his arm, staring at it in wonder.

"Shut the fuck up, bro," snapped Jason at the other wounded man. "You're not fucking blind."

Brent sighed and said to the healed soldier, "Excuse me."

"Sure," said the soldier. He rolled his shoulder to test it.

Brent now turned to the "blind" soldier who was sitting down next to the ruined truck. He bent to the man's face. "It helps if you open your eyes."

"I can't! They're stuck!"

Brent took out a simple rag from the pouches at his belt and wiped away the remaining blood. He staunched the wound on the man's head. He could have healed it, but he didn't feel that it was that big of an emergency. Sensing the soldier had no further injury, he said, "Try now."

The soldier's eyes popped open. He blinked a few times, looked up at Jason, then at Brent. "Hold this," Brent said, putting the rag in the man's hand. "Put it up here." He pulled the man's hand to his forehead.

"That's it?"

"That's it."

"Damn."

Brent walked back to his vehicle. Jason looked back at the soldier, gave him a shrug then followed Brent. The two men from the now-destroyed truck had to ride with someone, but Brent's Humvee didn't have the room. They instead went to the rear-most vehicle and hitched a ride with them back to camp.

Another truck in front of the blown-out truck had stopped, and would wait until a tow came for the ruined truck. If they left it out there, there would be nothing left by the morning, as the parts could be scavenged for use by the Taliban.

When they arrived at FOB Wilson, the platoon separated, most going to mess. Jason went with Custer to report to the Captain. Brent went to pick up mail.

Post was open 24/7, and the soldier behind the counter knew him by sight. "Hey, Brent," the soldier said. The postman retrieved a small package and an envelope for him. He frowned at the package — it usually meant new spells from the Archmagi. The envelope was addressed to him in fancy calligraphy.

6

He hurried back to his barracks. He was hungry, but mess would have to wait. The envelope with the calligraphy meant personal correspondence from the Archmagi.

The barracks tent had a few people in it. He shivered at the air conditioning. Nodding to the men there, he went to his cot. Brent dropped his items on the cot and got out of his tunic. He shivered again. After tossing the tunic aside, he sat on the hard cot and pulled out the calligraphic letter first. He carefully pulled up the flap that was taped down — magi did not expend their essence by licking envelopes. He pulled out the note. It was written in Enochian, the made-up language of Aleister Crowley and his Temple of the Golden Dawn. It only had one line at the top.

"Sign in twenty minutes or this letter will self-destruct. _____ "

"Dammit," he spat. He threw the letter down and turned to his foot locker. He fumbled with the lock, finally spelling it to snap open. He dug out a quill and ink, special items for articles like this. He inked the quill and scribbled his magical symbol on the line.

He waited. The letter shimmered. Appearing on the paper in English, in more calligraphy:

"You will be captured within the fortnight. They have the ability to kill you.

"The Archmage of CFT Thunder has been informed. Due to this, you will be on leave out of the country and must return to duty on July 12, 2004.

"Cybalia."

Cybalia, he thought, as the letter turned to dust, getting all over the bed. Cybalia was one of the most powerful clairvoyants in the entire armed forces. He'd met her once, when he got out of boot. She had said to him, "Heal the man named Parker, but he will die without you." Two weeks later, he healed a Private

Parker from the Third Infantry, but a week after that, the man had been shot through the eye from a ricochet.

Brent picked up the packet next. It notified him of his leave and contained a series of forms to fill out in triplicate. Another sealed envelope was included, typed up and addressed to Colonel Nosh.

His leave, according to the paperwork, was supposed to start as soon as a new mage arrived. The sooner he got this paper to Nosh, the sooner he would be let go.

Colonel Nosh was not going to be pleased. However, the fledgling Magic Corps was very particular about keeping their magi alive.

Brent pulled on his tunic, picked up the packet and his orders and headed toward Nosh's camp. He passed mess, sniffing the air. It smelled like garlic. His stomach growled.

Nosh's tent was air conditioned. He stopped for a moment at his secretary, who saw the envelope and his packet, then Brent's Magic Corps patch. She said, "He's already in there." He wondered what that meant.

He opened the door. Nosh sat behind a desk. The air conditioning was brutal in here. In front of Nosh stood a magus in full dark purple robes and pointed wizard hat. Brent hid his grin — this magus had gotten out of the academy recently, it seemed. All the magi wore the purple robes when they first graduated, but once they learned how unwieldy robes were in the field, they usually lost the robes and wore real uniforms.

This magus was older than both Nosh and Brent, but trim and fit. Brent studied the newcomer for a moment, noting his salt and pepper hair and soft brown eyes. *Will I look like that when I get older?* he thought, stopping himself from passing a hand through his own brown hair.

"You have those orders, Wizard?" demanded Nosh, holding out his hand without looking up at Brent.

"Yes, sir," Brent said, handing the packet and envelope over.

Nosh frowned, tearing open the envelope. "I don't need this shit right now," he muttered, unfolding the letter. "I send you out, I lose eight men. I keep you in, hundreds die."

Brent said, "With all due respect, sir, I don't think there's anything in there about other men being captured."

"The Taliban doesn't play POW games. They'll look at you and see the others as worthless."

"Then," said the older magus, "Send out eight men that you think are worthless."

Nosh snapped his head up to glare at the older magus. "You obviously have no idea that every man is worth it."

The older man shook his head. "I've been through this before, sir. Some men are more 'worth it' than others."

"All you magicians care about is yourselves."

Brent began, "Sir —"

Nosh looked up at him. "And you of all people have nothing to say about this."

"Yes, sir," said Brent quietly. Nosh held out the orders and a few other forms, signed while he had spoken. "First plane out of Kabul leaves tomorrow at 0300. You're on it."

"Yes, sir." He took the papers from Nosh.

"Now get out. Both of you."

The magi filed out after a salute. Brent glanced at the new magus. "You just get here?"

"Yes. Haven't even seen Q yet."

"Better get to that," Brent said. "Quartermaster's just past mess."

"Yes, sir," said the man, saluted, and left.

He finally got into mess, getting the remains of veal Parmesan and crusty ziti. As he ate, he kept his back to the wall, and could see the people walk around outside in the twilight.

He thought about the new magus. Was he a field mage? Could he protect the platoon like he did, or was he going to end up in the TOC, advising and seeing through the Fog of War?

The Magic Corps had been established in 1998, when the US Army discovered that magic actually worked. The Golden Dawn, Kabbalah, Ceremonial magic, the Key of Solomon and other grimoires had been proven over the years to be effective in war. At first considered a side interest of some pagan soldiers, the armed forces chose to codify the use of magic. Taking lessons from the Freemasons and other ceremonial magicians, grimoires, or magic books, were passed out to soldiers who had a strong will, could memorize long tracts of spells, and, most of all, believed in their own ability.

They also codified the ranks of the Magic Corps. Because the magi were across all the armed forces, they had to equate the ranks to the different armed forces. Beginning as Apprentices, they traveled through levels or "doors" as the Magic Corps called them. Brent was young for a First Magus. However, he had an edge.

The older magus he had met in Nosh's tent came into mess, his hair hidden by his new helmet. Wearing a regular uniform, he looked like a real soldier now.

Brent put aside what was left from his dinner and waited for the man to come over. The man saluted and said, "May I join you, sir?"

"Just finishing up," said Brent. "Sit down."

The magus sat, holding out his hand. "Martin Hesser."

"Brent Rogers," he said, taking it. "You're a little long in the tooth for the Corps."

"I've already done a tour for the Army years ago. Big Red One in Kuwait."

"Why are you here, then?"

"Suicide."

Brent furrowed his brow, confused.

"Bone cancer," said Hesser.

"Going out in a blaze of glory," Brent said, and Hesser nodded. "Maybe you can find something to live for here."

"I'm not worried," Hesser said. "If I do, I do. If not…I don't fit in back home. I hadn't for years."

"I wish you luck, Martin." He almost said what Hesser then said next:

"I'll be dead when you get back." He got up. "Good to have met you, sir." They shook hands again.

Brent sat back, not caring that Martin hadn't saluted him when he left. It didn't matter — he outranked him in the Army, being a first sergeant, but he was also a First Magus, a couple of steps away from an Archmagus, which equated to a lieutenant.

Brent got back to the barracks. He pulled out his backpack. Mark lumbered over while he was packing.

"Where the hell do you think you're going?" demanded Mark.

"Read it and weep," said Brent, tossing the orders on the bed.

"A month! You fucking bastard. You're going on leave for a month."

"Now?"

"Now," said Brent. "Plane leaves here at 0300."

Mark was fit to be tied, chewing on the air.

Brent looked up at him. "What's wrong?"

"We're gonna fuckin' die now," he said. Brent knew that the men were going to lose their edge.

TWO

✯ *WORCESTER, MONDAY* ✯

Logan Airport was busy at 5 a.m. on a Monday. Somehow Brent had lost a day in travel, but he slept most of it on the three planes that got him here.

He rented a car, took the insurance, and picked out a 2004 Chevy Impala. He caught Route 90, the Massachusetts Turnpike, while listening to a familiar Boston station playing Dire Straits. Worcester didn't have its own rock and roll radio station, so the airways had to pick up stations from the big cities of Boston and Providence, Rhode Island.

Familiar landmarks on Route 90 made him smile. Even the signs on the turnpike did: Allston/Brighton, Weston, Route 128, Framingham… I-495. Route 146, one of the Worcester exits.

He took that exit. From there, he continued to Route 122A, going to Worcester Center. Traffic was heavy around Worcester, due to signal lights and people trying to get to work early on Monday morning. He checked the clock in the car — it was near 8 a.m. Chances were his mother might still be home, getting ready for work, his father probably already at the police station for his job.

He drove to Edward Street, past the house. Still white siding, small for five, but too big for the remaining two. No cars were parked in the driveway, and the deck in the back had a mosquito net covering it. His heart gave a little leap — it was as he had left it. He continued down the street to the end, where it met MA-9. He took a sharp right, then another right into the parking lot of a large building which housed different doctors' offices for the University of Massachusetts Hospital across the street.

UMass Hospital, a sanctuary for vampires.

When he was 16, Brent had gone to work in the transport department in UMass, and met Dr. Bates, who openly stated he was a vampire. Vampires were legal in Massachusetts and most of the liberal New England states, but in other states, such as the Deep South, they were chased out at least, destroyed at worst. When Brent left for the Army, they were talking about making vampirism federally legal.

Brent walked into the medical building instead of the hospital, to the second floor, down the well-worn carpeted hallway, to the door that said, "Dr. Timothy M. Banant, Endocrinologist." Brent took a deep breath and opened the door. His hazel eyes lit immediately to the frosted sliding glass doors on the other side of the room. He went to the window and it took a moment before the glass slid open.

The woman with reddish-auburn hair and round glasses was looking at something on her desk as she asked, "Can I hel—" She looked up. Her jaw dropped.

"I was wondering if —"

"Brent!"

He grinned as she jumped up from her seat, ran around the desk and threw open the door that separated the office from the waiting room. Brent caught her in his arms when she ran into them. She was a petite woman, so catching her wasn't difficult.

"Hi, Mom," he said, hugging her. No one else was in yet. She stepped back a moment, looking up at him, her hazel eyes welling up with tears.

"Oh, my God, Brent — how — are —" She threw her arms around him again. "How long are you here?" she said, muffled in his uniform.

"About a month." Three weeks, four days to be exact.

"Why didn't you tell me?" She pulled back, putting her small hands on his biceps.

"I've been on planes since they gave me leave. I figured getting here was more important."

His mother looked him up and down. "They haven't been feeding you," she said. He knew he was fit and trim, hardly any fat on him at all. The Army did that to a person.

"Mom…"

"Did you call your father?"

"I thought I would go see him after I get a shower."

"You need the keys?"

"Um, yeah."

She walked back to the office. "Is Keithy still out of work?" he called.

"He was out last week."

Brent set his jaw, refraining from saying anything. His mother knew how he felt about Keithy and his "injury". Now was not the time or place to discuss it.

"I'll get these back to you at lunch."

"With a Ruben from Jake's."

He laughed. "Yes, Mom." His mother kissed him and sat down. An old man came in and held the door open for him. Brent murmured his thanks. He glanced at the old man, who smiled at him.

He walked to the car, and drove back to his parent's house. He unlocked the door to hear barking. The big German Shepherd came bounding out and leapt up, placing his huge front paws on Brent's shoulders.

"Pickles!" Brent rubbed the dog's head, scratching his ears, as the dog licked his face. Brent had hoped that Pickles would remember him. The two had been near inseparable since high school, when he got the German Shepherd. The K9 unit tried to train Pickles for basic work but he was the rebel of the litter. They finally put him up for auction and Brent's father won the bid.

"That's a good boy," he said, and the dog jumped down. He took off his backpack and set it down on the floor in the foyer.

He walked through the impeccably clean house to his room, as it was since he left but dusted frequently. The clothes he pulled out of his drawer smelled freshly laundered. He pulled out what he needed and got undressed.

Pickles was sniffing at his backpack. "Don't piss on it," Brent said, padding naked across the room to the door. He picked up the backpack, bringing it with him to the bedroom. After locking the front door, he walked over to the bathroom and took a long, much-desired hot shower. Finally, he wasn't encased in a layer of dust or dirt.

Pickles waited on his bed as he usually did. He and Brent played tug of war for a short time with the wet towel. Brent flipped the towel at Pickles who dove out of the way before it hit him. Brent pulled on his underwear. Those fit, however his denim shorts were a little too big. He chuckled as he threaded a belt through the hoops.

He pulled on an AC/DC t-shirt — it was a little tight across the chest, but still fit. He got on socks and sneakers.

He put Pickles out to the dog run. He stood at the credenza by the back door that held the fancy china, the set of dishes that were taken out for holidays. Along the top of the credenza were pictures of the family. In the center was his official Army picture in formal dress greens. He looked so young there, less than two years ago.

Keithy's picture showed a big broad man, his arm around Brent's shoulders. It was the last picture before the accident. Before Keithy stopped driving.

Another picture was of his sister, Lori. Her three kids were gathered around her, dressed in swimsuits, as she sat in a lounge chair by a nondescript pool somewhere. There were no pictures of her and her ex-husband, Alan, anywhere on the credenza.

When Pickles came back in, Brent made him pirouette before tossing a treat to him. "I'll be back, okay, big boy?" He found his old phone, plugged in the wall at his nightstand. He thought he was due for an upgrade by now. He unplugged it, flipped it open, and dialed the home landline. Hearing the home phone ring, he nodded, confirming that it worked.

Brent glanced at the clock on the phone. Nine. Plenty of time to see Dad. He flipped it shut and headed out to the car.

Brent parked in the tiny parking lot for visitors. He walked to the front of the building, built as a state of the art in the '70's but now rough around the edges like the men. As he got to the door, someone shut the door in his face. With an angry sigh, he tore the door open.

He walked into a foyer area lined with wooden benches on either side. The person who had slammed the door in his face sat at one bench, looking angry and nervous at the same time.

Brent walked up to the glass window and leaned on the counter. Beyond the window he could see officers both uniformed and plain-clothes, working. The desks and chairs beyond were metal and beaten, old and well-used, like a lot of the plain-clothes guys. The female officer talked to him through the small speaker set in the window. "Yes?"

"I'd like to see Detective Jim Rogers."

"In regards to?"

"I'm his son. From Afghanistan."

"I'll check if he's in. Please take a seat."

Brent sat down on the well-worn wooden benches across from the guy. The man glared at Brent, as if the reason he was here was his fault. Brent glared back at him, daring the guy to start something.

"What," the guy snapped at him.

"Nothing," said Brent, turning to look through the glass beyond the receptionist. This wasn't the first time he'd come to visit his father. A few of the uniforms glanced out at him, and one or two waved to him. He smiled and waved back.

He looked up to see his father moving on the left hand side of the room. He threaded his way between desks and came to the side door leading to the waiting area. Brent stood up to meet him. He was a large man, tall and broad like Brent, but with a paunch Brent didn't have. Because he was losing his hair, to make things easier, he went bald. He had Brent's angular face that was filling out, however; not as chiseled as his own.

"Brent!" He pulled Brent into a bear hug. "How are you? Are you here to stay?"

"Just a month," he said.

"At least for Fourth of July, that's good. Come on back."

People called him by name as he followed his father to a desk behind a partition and diagonally under the stairs. "I got a new partner. Luke gets in around 10." His father hooked a chair over for Brent. "Coffee?"

"As long as it's not the same that the Army has."

His father laughed. "Cream, no sugar?"

"Yep."

His father walked to the coffee station which was within view of the desk. Brent looked around — his father had moved from the middle of the room to the edge, closer to the glass-enclosed office of the captain of detectives. His father returned with the coffee, the stirrer sticking out of it. "How is it over there?"

"Do you want the line we're fed or the truth?"

"*Que est veritas,*" said his father. "What's in your gut?"

Leave it to his father to get right to the emotional heart of the matter. "It's a worthless fight. The people don't trust us, don't understand the idea of freedom and liberty. We're helping them so that the Taliban can come sweeping back to a clean country."

"Damn. You're there for how much longer?"

"Two years. Then college."

"Good thing you have plans. Better than your worthless brother."

"What's up with that?"

His father shrugged. "He's screwed the system, that's all. Got the right doctors to write the right things."

"Should I do some —"

His father said, "No. Leave him alone."

"I can cast something —"

"It's not worth it, Brent." He smiled and pointed to a small stack of files in a file holder on his desk. "At least my unsolveds are less than my solveds." He drank his own coffee. "Did you talk to your mother?"

"She wants lunch."

He chuckled.

"Hey, Brent." A man came over and clapped a pair of hairy hands on Brent's shoulders. "Back home?"

Brent craned his neck to look at the bear of a man standing over him. He was large in every sense, broad, strong, and hairy. "For a little while. Hi, Tony."

"Looking good, kid. The Army put some meat on those bones." He slapped Brent's shoulders, hard. Brent winced. "Captain wants us," he said to his father.

"Luke isn't in yet."

"Us." He motioned between Brent's father and himself. "As in you and me. We're the only ones here this early."

His father got up. "Must be a hot one. Be right back," he said to Brent.

Brent watched them go, his father walking over, swinging his arms, and Tony, loping along like the werewolf he was.

Rubbing shoulders with the vampires in UMass had introduced him to a whole host of Children of the Moon, as they liked to call themselves. Werewolves, vampires, fae, ghosts, and witches; creatures that most people didn't believe existed. Worcester was a stop for some of them on the way to Boston, where supposedly the RevWar ghosts and Old World vampires held sway.

Many of the Children of the Moon worked together. They believed that they were all of the shadowy underground, fringes of the multitudes of the Children of the Sun, as they called humans. As with the human races, countries, and cultures attempting to join with each other, there were some growing pains.

The fae's hate of the vampires had eased into dislike; the werewolves and vampires joined together and buried the hatchet centuries ago. Ghosts worked with anyone who could notice them, which were mostly witches and some vampires. Vampires liked to consider themselves the "aristocrats" of the Children of the Moon, but werewolves and fae often would put a kibosh on any vampire that got too big for their britches. That was when the old animosities would come into play, and a hunt would be called out on the vampire, who would have no recourse than to pipe themselves down or get out of Dodge before the wolves and fairies destroyed them.

Before he had even gone to UMass Hospital to work, sometimes Brent would help his father with cold cases. He glanced over at the file folders that his father had called "unsolveds." He lifted himself slightly off the chair and picked out the first folder from the pile.

Some of these cold cases were vampires that had lost control, or uncaring vampires that were passing through to Boston or other points beyond in the hinterlands of New York or even further west. Sometimes they were fights between werewolves, or a fae gone rogue. Or sometimes, they were just people.

He glanced around the room again, opened the folder. Taped to the inside flap were photographs, mostly of the scene of the crime. He wasn't looking for those. "Marilyn Monroe" was in the alias line, called that because she — he, actually — played that character in some clubs. He was found dead on Worthington Avenue, a hot spot for gays, drugs, and sex workers. His real name was unknown—

—*John Kemp*—

—Brent grabbed a sticky note pad and ball point, scribbled the name and pasted the note next to the blank spot that said "real name." He glanced around again, then continued to read the narrative.

"Marilyn" had been found dead from strangulation according to the coroner. He turned the page. Three suspects were named. He looked closely at each name, but none stood out. However, one of the suspects mentioned "Tool", and that name hi-lighted in red in his mind's eye.

All Brent had to do was think the spell, and "Tool" came up in his mind, everything from how he looked to his last known address, the make and model of his car —

Brent scribbled one note after another. He was still scribbling when his father snatched the folder out of his hands.

Brent's eyes were white when he noticed the folder was gone. To quench the spell, he closed his eyes and exhaled.

"I told you not to do that anymore," said his father sternly. "Psychometry isn't grounds for a warrant."

"Sorry, Dad." Brent opened his eyes. "I was only trying to help."

"I know you were. You've always been right. But this kind of thing is too freaky to admit in court. They don't care if the Armed Forces believes in it."

"Will you at least notify his next of kin?"

His father opened the folder and looked at the front page. "We'll try." He closed the folder and tossed it on his desk. "Besides, if the department knew what you could do, you'd be working for Larry first, and you know what kind of an idiot he is."

Brent glanced at an empty desk, a few rows away from his father's. Larry Salucci was an excellent patrolman, a mediocre sergeant, and a horrible detective. He never asked the right questions, even with a cheat sheet. He followed his gut, and was often wrong.

"Want to go with me on a call?"

Brent glanced at the clock. "Yeah, sure, I have a couple of hours."

"We'll bring you back in time for lunch." His father picked up his jacket.

Tony walked over to them, shrugging into his jacket. "Is Boy Wonder coming?" he asked.

"Yes. We have to bring him back for lunch or my wife will be pissed."

Tony chuckled. "C'mon then."

Brent climbed into the back seat. He searched for the buckles. "No seat belts?"

Tony turned to Brent's father. "What year is this car? 1967 Chevy?"

Brent found the seatbelt tucked into the back seat. "Never mind, I found them." His father drove the three of them to the hospital.

"Domestic violence," said Tony. "White female, aged 28, found beaten outside her home at four-thirty a.m. this morning. The newspaper delivery person called it in."

"You're going to be the reporter," said Brent's father to Brent. "Pick a paper."

"The *Gazette*?"

"Sold."

They drove to Saint Vincent's. They walked through the crowded emergency room, flashing their badges. Brent followed close so he wouldn't be left behind. The two men stopped at the nurse's station, and Tony asked where the woman was who had been found beaten. "Fifteen," said the nurse.

The three men went to the temporary room, separated from others by a thin wall of glass and curtains around it. The smell of the hospital reminded Brent of the operating theater back in Kandahar. All he needed to do was utter the healing spells he knew and most of these people would be out of here. But that would also mean he would be exhausted by the time he finished.

Brent's father knocked on the window, which was covered by a curtain. "Detectives Jim Rogers and Anthony Carlucci. Can we come in?"

"Yeah," said a tired voice, and the two men stepped inside. Brent came in right behind and took a spot in the corner.

The two detectives showed their ID. "I'm Detective Rogers," said his father. "What's your name?"

"Linda."

"Linda, can you tell us what happened?"

"Dunno," she said. Brent looked at the woman. Her eyes were swollen, one eye swollen shut, the other shiny and red. She was probably white, but her face was going to be covered in black and blue bruises. "Went outside with my dog. Got beat up. Don't know where my dog is."

Tony flipped open his reporter's notebook. "Do you live at 78 Lincoln Avenue?"

"It's my sister's house."

"Do you live there?"

"I was visiting."

"Where was your sister?"

"She's not home."

"What kind of dog do you have?"

"One of those mop top dogs."

"Havanese?"

"I guess."

Brent bit back a chuckle. Leave it to Tony to know his dog breeds

"What's your dog's name?"

"Harry."

His father asked, "Did your dog have a leash?"

"Yeah." She focused her open eye on Brent. "Who's that?"

"I'm a reporter from the *Gazette*," Brent said.

"I don't want no reporter here," said the woman. She glared at his father and Tony. "I don't know who beat me up and stole my dog."

"I thought you said you lost your dog."

"They musta stole my dog," she said.

They would eventually get her to tell them what was going on, but Brent wanted to help. Brent thought the truth spell and when the woman caught his eye, he let it go with a push of his will. The woman stared at him, blinking. The two detectives turned to look at Brent, who gave them a short nod.

"So," began Tony, "what —"

The woman suddenly burst into tears. "If I tell you, he'll kill him!"

"Who'll kill who?"

"Tyler. He'll kill my baby."

Her "baby" was Harry, the dog. She had gone outside to take the dog out while her sister wasn't home. Tyler had broken up a few days ago with her sister==who she refused to name. While Linda was outside, Tyler approached. Tyler, a linebacker training for the Patriots, easily overpowered her and started to beat her, first with a leftover snow shovel from outside, then with his fists. She tried to run to the door but he caught her in between the doorway and outside and he started beating her there too. She tried screaming, but the area was apathetic and no one came to her.

"He said he was gonna take my baby and he said he was going to kill him if my sister didn't talk to him."

Brent stepped outside, having "gotten the story." His father asked more questions as Tony stepped out to take a look at the records. Brent hung around the room, until his father came out. "Need to see if the dog's still there," he said.

Tony returned. "No note of a dog following the ambulance."

"Of course not. That would be too easy."

Tony chuckled. "I shouldn't have a hard time finding a dog."

"The hard time will be if the dog goes to you, Tony."

"Just because I'm an alpha doesn't mean I can get all dogs to do what I want."

They arrived at Lincoln Avenue. Brent's dad got out of the car and walked around the crime scene while Tony asked the neighbors if they heard anything. When he knocked on the door of one apartment, he heard a dog barking.

"Small dog," said Tony. Some locks clicked open and the door opened a crack. A middle-aged black woman looked out. Tony showed his badge. "Do you know a Linda Sunder?"

"Is she okay?" asked the woman. "She didn't bring in her dog." The woman opened the door and the little dog wove between her feet, stopping short at seeing Tony.

"Is this her dog?"

"Yeah. I saw'm outside. Poor thing."

Tony smiled, reached down to pet the dog, but the animal yipped and jumped away. Brent knew that he would have that kind of reaction. Tony was the alpha wolf of his pack, after all.

Brent watched Tony ask the questions. Tony easily filled the door frame with his broad shoulders. He had joined the force only four years ago, coming from New Hampshire. He told them right away that he was a werewolf. Under the guise of diversity, they hired him. But only a few people, including Brent's dad, would work with him.

Tony finished up, thanking the woman, and promising to tell Linda that she had her dog. Tony and Brent met Brent's father outside.

"We found the dog," said Tony.

"We have to get you back to the station," said Brent's father to Brent. "So you can go get your mother's lunch."

Brent looked at his watch — it was already 11:30. "Oh, yeah."

"Having fun?" Brent's dad asked, getting into the car.

"Yeah. I kind of miss this."

"We don't tell the boss, right?" said Tony.

"Of course not," said Brent's father, putting the car in drive.

Brent parked his rental at the far end of one of the last remaining dining cars in New England. A silver bullet placed in the middle of a parking lot, Jake's was a breakfast and lunch grill. At this time of day, it was going to start picking up for the lunch crowd.

Jake Junior saw Brent when he came into the diner. "Hey!" Jake was Brent's age, set to inherit the family business, if it survived.

The two men shook hands, but Jake pulled Brent into a brief hug. "How the hell are you?" Jake asked.

"Good. You?"

"Meh. What can I get you?"

"Two Rubens, the original way."

"You got it, man." Jake hobbled back behind the counter. He had been born with one leg slightly shorter than the other, so he always hobbled. Brent sat down at the counter. A waitress gave him a glass of water.

Brent watched the clientele through the mirrors that lined the wall between the kitchen and the counter. He felt that the very few people there watched him suspiciously. They reminded Brent of the people in Kabul.

"How long are you in this part of the world?" called Junior.

"About a month," Brent said.

"I got your picture, by the way." He pointed to the picture wall that had pictures of all sorts of locals in different locales, from Disney World to fishing. He didn't see it in the mess of pictures on the wall.

"Great," said Brent. He turned in his seat to match eyes with a hobo that sat in the corner, staring at him intently. The beginning of a demand spell started in his mind, but he shut it down. The man was probably schizophrenic and suspicious of him.

"You want to work here when you get back?" asked Jake, peering over the back counter's shelf.

"Not really." The hobo bothered him, so he put up a protection spell around his person. The spell was strong enough to bounce off bullets or a speeding train. He'd tried the former with excellent success, but didn't trust it enough to stand in front of a train to see if it would bounce off.

"You love to cook," Jake continued.

"What the hell gave you that idea?"

Jake laughed. Another person came in. Brent looked at the newcomer's hands. They weren't carrying anything or holding extra fabric from their clothes, trying to hide a bomb.

God, he had to relax.

Jake finished the Rubens. He put the two styrofoam containers in a plastic bag and brought them over as Brent dismissed the protection spell. "Enjoy. Come back for breakfast tomorrow, we can catch up. On the house."

"With an offer like that, I'll be here when the doors open."
He waved at Jake.

The hairs on the back of his neck prickled. He stopped for
a moment and turned around. The hobo was still staring at
him.

He's not going to do anything. He's probably crazy. Brent
got in the car, still watching the man, even to the last moment
that he pulled out of the parking lot. He sighed, calming himself
down.

He was better by the time he got to the doctor's office. His
mother was greeting a patient. She saw Brent when the patient
stepped away from the frosted glass. "Be right there, honey,"
she said, smiling.

A few minutes later, she opened the door for him to come
in back. Among the mess of papers and files, phones and
computers, he saw the two women who worked with the doctor
— a nursing assistant named Tina and the medical records and
assistant secretary, Michelle. He said hello to them. They
smiled and waved.

His mother brought him to the break room in the back
that consisted of a refrigerator and a table with two waiting
room chairs that had seen better days. "Was your father busy?"

"He went on a call."

"You didn't go with him, did you?"

"No, Mom." His mother wouldn't like it and be worried if
he told her the truth. One time, when he was still in high
school, his father had brought him into a drug-infested area of
Worcester on a call. Although he survived and was fine, she
never forgave him for it.

Brent handed over the top styrofoam box. "I got the same
thing as you, Mom." She smiled and took her box.

"I might go to see Keithy after this," he said, opening his
box. A grilled corned-beef sandwich on rye with a huge load of

29

fries that nearly overflowed the box looked delicious. "Anything I should expect?"

"Like?" His mother hesitated to take a bite.

"I don't know. A wife, a baby?"

She took a bite. "A widow was employing him as a handyman for a little while until he couldn't do it anymore. No, nothing like that."

Brent took a bite of the sandwich. He hoped its wonderful taste would calm him down. It didn't, not quite.

"Brent, he's good at what he did, it's just —"

"He's a sociopath and a con artist," snapped Brent. "He's good at that."

His mother sighed.

Brent did also. "Look, I'm sorry. After what he pulled on you…"

"That wasn't his fault."

He set aside his sandwich. "Mom. He took the retirement money from you and Dad and blew it on a casino."

"He invested it in stocks."

"Same thing, Mom. The company tanked and you both lost everything," If he had been home, he would have been able to stop them from doing it. But Keithy hooked in the entire family on a tech startup that failed utterly a year later.

"Your father forgave him. Why can't you?"

"Keithy came out smelling like a rose." Keith had not put money in the same tech company that he dumped the retirement money in, but bought another tech company that went public. This one was called "Apple" and it took off like a rocket. Brent waved his hand. "Forget it. I didn't come here to get all riled up over Keithy."

"How's your sandwich? Good, isn't it?"

He had eaten half of it without tasting it. "Yeah, it is," and forced himself to taste it this time. It was good, but not like he remembered it.

"Did you get the letters from your sister?" asked his mother around bites.

"I get them. I've been emailing her."

"It's not the same," said his mother.

"Mom, we don't have a lot of downtime." Lori was lucky she was getting emails.

"She said that she would send you letters every day if you want. You know that Kaitlyn is in school? She'll probably be writing you, too."

"Lori still have the home day care?"

Her mother brushed off the remaining rye crumbs. "No, she got rid of that a while ago. She got someone to watch the kids and she works over here at UMass at night."

He jerked upright. "At night?"

"Three to eleven shift. She works in the laundry. It's only part time…"

He had worked the three to eleven shift, too, when he was in high school. He had been exposed to the UMass Hospital's underbelly. He knew the predators that were there. "I thought she said she'd rather die than work for UMass."

"Funny how things change." She gave him a look. "Like someone who was going into the National Guard and went full-on into the Army instead."

"Touche'," he said, tossing the styrofoam box in the plastic bag.

"You're going to stay home tonight?"

"I should be home for dinner."

"I have some left over roast beef and potatoes and a recipe for hash."

He smiled. His mother always had a recipe for something and loved to inflict it on the family. *God, I missed this.* "The Army has taught me to eat whatever is put in front of me, even if it's still wiggling."

She laughed and got up, gathering her box from lunch. She escorted him back to the waiting room. She stood on tip toes, gave him a quick kiss and said, "Don't let Keithy get to you."

Easier said than done, he thought.

Brent sat outside of Keithy's apartment on the south side, debating whether to visit him or not. Surrounding the apartment were other homes that looked similar, triple-deckers that had been built in the '50's to house people who worked in the mill nearby. Now the mill was dead, and the surrounding area had gone to pot, with drug dealers on the corner and probably whores at night. During the day, it didn't look that horrible. During the day, he didn't mind parking the rental there.

Brent thought that Keith, the oldest of the Rogers children, would be a good role model for the rest of the children to follow. He could be good, if he cared about someone other than himself.

Starting when Brent was very young, Keith would take Brent's money, clothes and toys, and call them his own, give them away as if they were his own, and would even put his name on them. He often played the victim, which his mother would give in to; Keith was never the bully, but was the one who was getting beaten. Brent didn't know if these things were true or not, but every year Keith would get some kid in trouble in school.

After school, he couldn't hold down a job because other people would fall for his charms and then get burned. He had the Rogers' good looks, with an open face and wide, soft brown eyes. He had women, a new girl every season, it seemed. Then came the accident.

The van Keith was driving got hit and he spun around, half in the median and half on the shoulder, facing oncoming traffic. Keith said that he had Post Traumatic Stress Disorder and claimed he couldn't drive or even get in another car. Some doctor agreed, and now he was trying to get disability payments from the government. Taking his family's money had been the last straw.

The more Brent thought about it, the angrier he got.

Brent got out of the car and looked up at the wooden porches on the three floors of the house. He walked around back and in through a side entrance. He checked the mailboxes first. K. Rogers, 2nd floor. Brent nodded to himself and climbed to the second floor.

He knocked, a gentle rap at first, then harder.

"Yeah, wait a minute," came a voice from the inside. Brent heard someone moving on the other side of the door. He put his hand on the door and was going to cast the spell to see what was beyond the door when it opened.

A much younger and fatter version of his father, with brown hair like his own and deep brown eyes like his father's, stood in the doorway dressed in only a pair of undone jeans. He had gained weight since Brent had last seen him.

"Hey," Brent said.

Keithy buttoned his pants. "Hey."

They stood like that for a while. Neither moved to hug or even shake hands. Brent finally said, "Can I come in?"

"You gonna hit me?"

"What gave you that idea?"

"You told Lori in an email that you would beat the crap out of me the next time you saw me."

"A fit of passion," said Brent.

"Look, it's not my fault about the money."

"I'm not here to talk to you about that." Brent stuffed his hands in his pockets, to stop himself from even motioning a spell.

Keithy stepped aside to let Brent in, and he stepped into a dining area with a table with three chairs. Just beyond was the living room, and beyond that was a door out to the porch. To his left was the bathroom, and another room leading off from the living room — probably the bedroom. The apartment looked clean, too clean for Keithy, who hardly ever cleaned his own room. "What are you here for, then?" asked Keithy.

"I was in the neighborhood."

"So are you home for good?"

"No. On leave."

"For how long?"

"A month or so."

"Wanna beer?"

"Sure."

Keithy shuffled over to his fridge in the kitchen located parallel to the door he had entered. The kitchen held the refrigerator and stove, and a small countertop that was covered with assorted kitchen small appliances. "If I knew you were coming, I would have gotten snacks."

"I only found out two days ago, and I was on planes here for 30-something hours."

Keithy returned with two Coronas, handing one to Brent. He waved to the living room that had a leather couch and a flat screen TV on the wall. "Still out of work on comp?" asked Brent.

"Yeah." Keithy shivered. "Nightmares."

Brent narrowed his eyes. "Are you kidding? A little car accident on the highway and you've got *nightmares*?"

"You don't believe how bad things are. I can't drive anymore."

"That's bullshit. A truck blew up in front of me just a couple of days ago. You don't see me not driving because of it."

Keithy drank the beer. "That's your job. Some people are stronger than others." He looked pensively at his beer. "I know I'm a coward."

"You don't have to pull the victim act in front of me."

"Act? You think I'm acting?"

Brent took a deep drink of the beer to stop himself from going off on his brother. *Yes, I think you're acting. I think this is all bullshit so you can get money from the government, just like you get money from everyone else.*

The apartment door creaked open. A short woman, her brown hair in a ponytail and wearing a t-shirt and shorts peered into the apartment. He could see her face, small but angular, with a perky nose and thin lips. She carried grocery bags in both hands, as she used them to push her way into the apartment. "I'm back," she called, and struggled into the apartment. Keithy and Brent both stood up to help her. Keithy moved a little faster than Brent, however.

"Thanks so much, Chrissie. I don't know what I'd do without you." He shut the door as Chrissie manhandled the groceries onto the kitchen table.

"Oh, no bother. I was going that way."

Brent stepped into the dining room. "Chrissie," said Keithy when Chrissie looked up at Brent, "This is my brother Brent. He's come home from Afghanistan."

Brent crossed the room. "Hello, Chrissie."

"You were in the war?" she asked, shaking his hand.

"Still am. I'm only here for a little while."

"He's one of those magicians," said Keithy.

Chrissie's eyes widened. "You are?"

Brent shot Keithy a look, knowing what was going to happen next. *Can you do any tricks?*

She surprised him, however. "Do you hurt people with magic?"

"Sometimes," he said.

"Kill them?"

"I try not to."

"But I bet there's collateral damage," said Keithy.

Brent glared at him. Brent remembered writing "collateral damage" more than once in his career. He had learned to minimize it. "I try not to," Brent said again.

"That must be so interesting. Doing magic," she said.

Brent shrugged. "It comes easy to some people. Others are bare-bones magi." He thought of Martin, still in his robes out of the academy, obviously armed with the bare minimum of spells, how he would be dead in a week.

"What's that mean?"

Keithy butted in. "I'm going to need help putting these away."

"Huh? Oh, sure."

Brent bit back a warning. Did she know how his victim-act only got people to think he needed help? He didn't have to be a magus to see the jealousy dripping from Keithy.

Keithy had Chrissie put away most of the groceries, while Brent found his way back to the living room and examined the videos in stock. Most were horror, not Brent's taste. A couple were rom-coms, which surprised him, but Brent assumed they were for any girl he invited over. The x-rated ones were in a cabinet at the bottom, most multiple girls on one guy. *Typical fantasy*, Brent thought, but his fantasy involved men in addition to the girls.

Brent looked up when they were almost done and ready to part ways. "Hey, Chrissie," he called.

"Yeah?" She smiled at him.

"Are you busy tomorrow night?"

She put a hand on her hip. "Why, Brent. I think you're asking me out."

"Dinner. Is Lucky's still open?"

"Yes," she said. "I'd love to go."

"Where and when do you want me to pick you up?"

"I live nearby," she waved to the left. "Is four too early?"

"Four it is. I'll see you then."

"Pick me up in front here. I'll be ready." She smiled at him and left.

Keithy glared at Brent. "Thanks. Thanks a lot."

"What?"

"I've been trying to get in her pants for months now and you'll probably leave her place on Wednesday morning."

Brent finished his beer and handed Keithy the empty. "I'll be going."

Keithy snarled at him, "When you start suffering from nightmares of 'collateral damage', I'll laugh in your face."

"At least I'll have a better reason than being in a fender-bender."

"It wasn't a fender-bender!" Keithy yelled.

"Right," Brent said.

He left his brother's apartment on Southgate Street, heading back to Main Street. Brent eventually found his way to Scandinavia Avenue. His sister's two-bedroom was above a hair salon. Her car was parked in the lot in back, an old black Mercedes from before she was married. Her pride and joy, Black Sunshine had recently become a sinkhole for repairs. Brent parked his car next to it.

He walked to the back of the building and up a set of outdoor wooden stairs. He hesitated at her door, and put his hand on it. He muttered the spell to see in his mind's eye beyond the door:

—*his sister standing in the kitchen, watching the TV, a mug in her hand*—

He removed his hand and knocked. He looked up at the peephole to give her a good view; he heard a squeal on the other side of the door, fumbling as locks and bolts came undone. She threw open the door and almost fell into his arms. "Brent!"

"Lori," he said and hugged her tight.

"When did you get here?" she asked, pulling away.

"This morning. You, as usual, are the last to know."

"As usual. Come in. Coffee?" Her reddish-brown pony tail bounced as she walked. She was thin like Brent, though when she was younger she was all arms and legs like a colt. She had since grown into her skin and her face, angular like the rest of the Rogers' clan, was more open and didn't hide any emotions like the boys could do. She had gotten that from her mother. She was older than him by one year, younger than Keithy by three.

"Coffee sounds great."

Her apartment was all white. He supposed that made things easier for the landlord, but it was difficult to remain clean with three kids. He walked down the short hallway to her kitchen, which looked out into the living area, not quite unlike Keithy's apartment. However, her living space was much smaller, with three bedrooms. One bedroom was off the living room, and two bedrooms were down another hallway that led off from the living area.

There were dents and scratches in the walls. In many of the areas of the walls, were light marks of orange, green, or blue, where the kids had used the walls for murals and Lori tried to wash off the damage.

"Extra light, no sugar?"

"You remembered."

She turned off the TV and poured him a cup with a liberal amount of fake cream. "How's Army life treating you?"

"I can't complain."

"Did you ever?"

"It's not worth it to. And I complained a hell of a lot in boot."

"Bull. 'My ass hurts.' 'They make me carry shit up walls! I'm a mule!'"

He smiled, sipped his coffee. "Did you memorize my emails?"

"And what about after that?" She sat on her threadbare couch, tucking her leg under her. He took the recliner that had so much stuffing sticking out of it that he wondered if there as any stuffing left.

"I went into the Magic Corps."

"Did that work out?"

"A lot of the spells," he said, "are intelligence-gathering. Sensing if something is 'off' around you. Then if you can handle that, they teach you offensive or defensive spells."

"Let me guess. You're offensive."

"Bingo. Lots of built-up power in here." He tapped his chest.

"I thought when Oompa died, you calmed down."

Oompa, their grandfather, had died of a heart attack right in front of Brent. "I saw what being high-strung and hot-tempered did to Oompa, and I didn't want to go down that road." He drank the cooling coffee. "But the Army — it can bring out the worst in people."

She gathered both of her legs up under her. "Why didn't you tell me?"

"Because the emails are censored and read by other magi. It's classified stuff."

"I'm not asking for spells," she said.

He shrugged. "I know. Where are the kids?"

"Day care until six. The state pays for it, so why not?" She sipped her coffee. "Do you like being a…what is it, a magician?"

"Magician is the common term in the Army, but magus is what the Corps prefers. A lot of times I'm called Wizard or Warlock."

"Do you like it?"

"I'm a master sergeant, Lori, something I could never be if I was in standard infantry. In two years, I rose six ranks due to my power, ability, and track record. You leave with me in a team, I make a point to bring you home alive. Sometimes injured, but alive."

She had a small smile.

"What?"

"The Army sure gave you pride."

"It's the truth." He bristled.

"I don't doubt that it is," she said. "But something tells me you could walk up to Sarah's fiancé and punch Boz in the face without a problem."

"He's her fiancé?" He slowly set down the coffee cup.

"She showed me the ring on Valentine's Day. Next summer, she said."

His stomach lurched, both on fire and a deep, bottomless pit threatening to swallow it whole. He had been so in love with Sarah, but in their senior year, she broke up with him. He pined for her, wrote letters to her, begged for her to take him back. Now she was going to marry Boz, the first guy she rebounded to after breaking up with him.

"Would you?" asked Lori.

"Would I what?"

"Hurt him?"

He shrugged. "I don't know." He did know, though.

She smiled and gathered the coffee cups. "Take the high road," she said. "You staying with Mom and Dad?"

"Yeah. My clothes don't fit." He showed her the belt.

"Maybe we can go out tomorrow."

"I have a date tomorrow night."

"Ohhhh?" She grinned. "It was the uniform, right?"

"I wasn't in uniform."

"That explains it."

Brent stood up to hide the blush. "Stop that, Lori."

She laughed, taking the cup from the table. She got up to put the cups in the sink. "A date. With who?"

"Keithy's new squeeze."

"You saw Keithy? You didn't —"

"Not to say I didn't want to hurt him, but when push came to shove, I was the one who walked away."

"The Army's good for something," she said.

"Possibly that." He put his hands behind his back, parade rest. "She was more interested in what I'd done than what magic I could do."

"Same thing. This the girl from the third floor?"

"No, next door, she said."

"Oh. He's going after the girl upstairs."

"You've seen this?"

"So has Mom. Mom goes over with some money every week."

Brent sighed.

"I know. I make sure he pays the bills with it, because you know him."

"He probably told Mom he'd pay her back after the settlement."

"Of course he did. I go with Mom because you know how she is, too."

"She'd give him her paycheck." He turned to look out the window. "How can Keithy be like that to his own mother?"

"Someday it'll catch up to him. Then we'll laugh, but it'll break Mom's heart."

"Yeah," said Brent, looking back at Lori. "So what about you? No man in the picture?"

She giggled. "I was talking to Dr. Bates from anesthesiology. He says he knows you."

Brent focused his eyes on the counter, trying not to let his body betray his feelings. "Dr. Bates and I used to talk a lot. About the future. He suggested I join the military."

"He had the right idea," she said, washing the cups. It hurt him to lie to his sister, but he didn't want to drag her into the nether world that he inhabited. He'd protect her with his life from it.

"You shouldn't get involved with him."

"Why?"

Brent shook his head. "He's married to his work." He wanted to tell her the truth: *He's a vampire.*

She shrugged, set the coffee mugs in the strainer. "I'm sort of seeing someone anyway. Remember Chuck Ashford?"

"That manager in the mall?"

"The Gap. That's him."

"Friend with benefits?"

She blushed and threw the first thing that came to hand — the towel. His eyes widened, the spell formed in his mind, and the towel exploded into fine threads that rained on the counter and floor.

She stared at him. He stared at her.

"What did you go and do that for?" he demanded.

"I thought — I thought you were going to catch it."

"You wanted me to perform a trick? All you had to do was ask."

"I'm sorry, Brent, I don't know why I did that."

He waved his hand, and the threads from the destroyed towel flowed up from the floor onto the counter, gathering into a neat pile. "Remember, I'm an offensive mage. My first instinct is to destroy it."

Shaking, she swept the towel into a trash can. He had ruined the mood, which was nothing new.

"I'm going to go," he said, "Before I bend your cutlery."

"Come back tomorrow, Brent. We'll go shopping before your date." She gave him the "puppy dog eyes" look that always turned his heart soft.

He sighed.

She said, "I get it. I'm sorry."

He pulled out his keys. "Enough already." He walked without an escort down the short hallway to the door.

Brent wanted to get out of Lori's apartment before the kids got home. He did not like children, especially Lori's. Ever since her divorce, they ruled the roost. The youngest, Dante, at his terrible threes, was the worst and needed a good beating in Brent's opinion. The kid was smart and manipulative, not too unlike his uncle Keith. He looked different than the other children, with dark hair and eyes, versus the blond and blue eyes of the girls. Dante had Spanish blood in him somehow.

It was still early, 3:30 in the afternoon, so he drove around a while, taking in the sights and sounds of his old stomping grounds. He found himself at the Red Bar, a place the cops frequented.

Located three blocks from the station, the Red Bar was often the first place to go before or after a shift. Its faded red awning surrounded the perimeter of the two-floored building and gave the bar its name. The second floor had four tenants above the bar, that were quiet and complacent.

He had gone in there with his dad a few times or to go get his dad. This was back in the day when bartenders didn't have to worry about underage kids in their bar.

He parked in the lot and walked inside. It hadn't changed in the two years he'd been away. The bar was set at the side of the room, two seats wide by eight seats long. The mirror was polished to a fine sheen and reflected Brent as he walked up to the bar. Third shift cops drank their morning cocktail, retirees watched the news with armchair commentary, and the bartender behind the bar ruled it all.

Brent sat down at the bar, a couple of seats away from what seemed to him to be a serious alcoholic. The bartender sauntered up to Brent. "Birch beer," Brent said.

The bartender chuckled. "Still on duty?" He got an amber bottle out and popped the top. He set a glass down next to it, but Brent waved it away and took a pull from the bottle.

"You could say that."

"It's always five o'clock some'ere," muttered the drunk.

Brent glanced at him, taking the man in. He thought of the spell, and listened to the inner voice that told him more than he needed to know about this man.

- Mark Pearson

- has to work tonight and doesn't care how sauced he gets —
hopes that a drug dealer takes him out -

"What you starin' at, kid?" Pearson demanded.

"Nothing, sorry." He'd stared too long, made it noticeable.

"What'chu want?"

"Nothing. I said I'm sorry."

"That's not good enough," said the drunk, and slid off the stool, not able to stop himself. His feet hit the floor but his legs buckled, and he grabbed the bar next to him to keep himself upright.

Brent sighed. "I don't want a fight."

"Neither do I," said the bartender, suddenly out from behind the bar, and now behind Pearson. The bartender grabbed Pearson's arms, and basically frog-marched him out. "Come back when you're sober, eh?"

"Fuck you. Maybe I won't be back."

"No skin off my nose," said the bartender, tossing him out and heading back behind the bar.

Brent watched the door, to see if Pearson was going to come back in. The bartender didn't seem to mind, and racked up another birch beer. The bartender said, "He's usually not that…"

"Belligerent? It was probably me. I have that effect on people."

"Heh." He regarded Brent. "I don't think I've seen you here before."

"I'm Jim Rogers' son."

"Oh, Jimmy. I know Jimmy. You're the one who won't come out of the house because of some car accident?"

"That's my brother, Keith."

"Then you're the one who went overseas."

"That's me."

"Iraq?"

"Afghanistan."

"Should have said something. I would have given you real beer."

Brent held up the bottle. "On duty, remember?"

"Next time when you're not."

"Deal," Brent said, and drank from the second bottle. "I'm surprised that home is this friendly."

"People fucked up after Vietnam. They don't want to do it again. But I know a few liberal cops who think the war was a mistake."

Brent shrugged.

"You hear about all the ex-military guys going off. They can't make it in civilian life."

"That's what the VA is for. Provide support and assistance for those who need to come back to civilian life."

"Are you back home permanently?"

"No, just visiting."

"Do you miss it?"

"Miss what?"

"The war."

Brent drank, to give himself a moment. "To be honest, I don't know. I miss the risk. I miss my platoon. I miss working with the people there."

"At least you're honest. You could always become a cop."

"So a soldier would be better off as a cop, you're saying?" Brent laughed. "I see what my dad has to go through, the hoops he has to jump. I don't see myself going through that."

"These guys are a band of brothers, like you," said the bartender, in all seriousness. "Sometimes these guys need someone who's got their backs. The minute they fuck up once, the media has a field day with them and they got Internal Affairs after them."

"Which is one reason I can't be a cop. Too much internal shit." He set down his empty bottle. "I'd better head out. I'll be back sometime."

"You're welcome here any time, man."

Brent sat back, holding his stomach. "There's more corn," his mother said.

"I can't, Mom. Seriously, I can't." The kitchen table was laden with enough food to feed a platoon. His mother made the hash with eggs. And corn. And string bean casserole. And potato pancakes.

"You hardly ate anything."

"Maggie," said his father, "They don't feed you enough to begin with."

"I bought a cream pie, too."

Brent groaned. "Maybe later, Mom."

His father sat back, lighting a cigarillo. "Did you see Keith and Lori?"

"Yes," Brent said. "Oh, that reminds me, I have a date tomorrow night."

"Already?" asked his mother.

"That's my boy!" said his father, laughing.

Brent chuckled. "Already."

"Not Sarah," said his mother.

"No."

"She's engaged now."

"Lori told me."

"You should have told Lori to come by with the kids."

"I wanted to spend my first night alone with you."

"Not only did the Army teach him how to fight," said his father, "but gave him a honeyed tongue as well."

"Magic school did that."

There was a long, uncomfortable pause. Did his parents not like him going into magic? Finally, his mother said, getting up, "Since there won't be any pie, I'll clean up."

"Let me do it, Mom." When he got up, Pickles rose from under the table and looked at him expectantly. "It's the least I can do since I'm staying here."

She glanced at her husband, who only smiled with pride. She made a big to-do about sitting down. Brent gathered the dishes and brought them to the sink.

HIs parents were talking quietly between themselves as Brent washed. With a murmur of sounds, he set the simple listening spell in place:

"...he'd be fine." His father.

"But they get hurt there all the time."

"He's one of those magicians. They don't die, so they say. If you try and kill one, you get cursed or something."

"How do you know that?" His mother's voice was full of worry.

"Maggie, trust him. Trust in the Corps. He'll be fine."

Brent decided that he should tell them why he was here, when the doorbell to the back door rang, making Pickles jump up, barking. His father answered the door. Brent heard, "Hey, how's it going?"

"Not bad, Mr. Rogers. We heard Brent's back."

"Come in. Brent, you have visitors."

Brent put the last plate on the strainer. He glanced at the door. "Hey, George."

George stood about Brent's height, so their brief hug was at the same level. Brent noticed he had a paunch now. His brown eyes sparkled, and he had his customary five-o-clock shadow. His short black hair looked uncombed, as usual.

Behind him came Matt, a shorter but well-built blond. His blue-grey eyes took Brent in before he gave him a hug. These were the guys he ran with at high school.

The three of them got together before and after school, got their licenses together, had gone to concerts and even sometimes on dates with their girls together. After the "Hey, how goes?" banter, George asked, "Want to play pool?"

"Old Man Black's place?" asked Brent, fondly remembering the good old days in Old Man Black's pool hall.

"Yeah. He serves us liquor now."

"I promised to stay here."

His father waved a hand. "You boys go on. We'll be fine."

"Ok. I need to get home early, though."

"You still got a curfew?" asked George and Matt laughed.

"My mom won't go to bed if I stay out too late." He kissed his blushing mother and followed the guys outside. Brent smiled when he saw the dark green car, held together by Bondo and spit. "Still driving that piece of shit Mazda?"

"Gets me where I wanna go," said Matt. "You can ride shotgun, Brent."

Brent pushed down the seat and George climbed into the back, muttering, "Why do I have to go in the back?" Matt pulled out of the lot and took a left back onto Main. "Miss being home?" asked George.

"Yeah," said Brent.

"Not when he's got a curfew," said Matt.

"The Army has a curfew too, so I'm used to someone else telling me what to do with my time."

"What about those Afghan chicks?" asked George, "They all fat under those sheets?"

"*Burqas*," said Brent.

"Whatever."

"They're like everyone else, I guess. Not all the women wear that. Some just wear the *hajib*."

"The what?"

"The scarf that covers the head."

"Doesn't it get hot?"

Brent shrugged. "Maybe."

Said George, "I bet they have nothing on underneath."

"Everything is cotton. Besides, I didn't come here to explain Islamic culture."

"But what about the chicks, man?"

Brent sighed. "They're like ours." But a lot tougher and a little more scared.

"Did you get laid over there?"

"Not yet. Jesus, George, you thinking with your dick, tonight?"

Said Matt, "Ever since Miranda dumped him, he's—"

"Fuck you, Matt. Tim-oh-thee probably showed her his dick and she got all hot and bothered, when she kept telling me, 'We're going to wait until we're married.'"

Brent asked, "Tim-oh-thee anyone I know?"

"No," said Matt "Told you way back she was a lying sack of shit. 'Wait 'til we're married' is code for 'you ain't gettin' none, son.'"

Brent laughed, but George looked pissed off. The bar's parking lot was pretty busy for a Monday night. "Bosox game?" asked George, after they got out of the car.

"Tournament?" asked Brent.

"Wrestling," said George. "Or a party. Welcome home!" He put an arm around Brent's shoulder and squeezed. Brent shoved him gently away.

The parking lot betrayed how busy the bar was. Three TVs had wrestling, two TVs had closed-captioned ESPN. The bar at the edge of the room was full, but the tables surrounding it and at the base of the TVs were empty. Old Man Black was manning one end of the bar, and his bouncer stood menacingly on the other end. Across from the bar was a raised section with six pool tables.

They mounted the three steps to the pool tables, which were empty. They picked a table in the corner next to the rest rooms. "I'll get us a pitcher," said George.

"Careful of him," said Matt quietly. "He'll drink the whole pitcher on his own."

Brent nodded. George seemed "off" tonight. George came back, the pitcher and three glasses in hand, as Matt started racking up the balls. They flipped to see who would play first. Brent didn't force the throw, and lost.

Matt picked up the stick from the wall and bent over to break. Brent, drinking his weak beer, watched George drink glass after glass. Soon enough, the beer was gone, the game over, with George losing. Brent paid for the second pitcher, while George got a few shots of whiskey in addition to the beer.

Matt switched off the beer after the first pitcher, Brent stopped after the second. George was going to get a third pitcher until Brent told him he'd be drinking it himself. By this time, though, George was feeling good already, with a pitcher of beer and about six shots of whiskey in his system. Brent was happy Matt was sober.

Brent had won the last game, and George was going to play against him. Brent was going to break, when he looked up from the pool table and saw Boz. Brent stood up, knowing that if he tried to break now, he would explode the other balls with the cue ball.

Matt looked across the room where Brent was looking. "Aw man," he moaned.

Boz was laughing at something one of his friends was saying. Brent was never able to take him in high school, but with Army training, he probably could. The linebacker was still broad and big. However, now, with magic training, he could hurt the bastard who he believed stole his girlfriend.

"Dude," said George, looking in the same direction, "It's been, what, three years?"

A lonely senior year, and two more lonely years in Afghanistan. They didn't understand, did they? They hadn't been in love. They hadn't known what she meant to him. He couldn't tell them that he planned on marrying her, spending the rest of his life with her; and now, now this drunk was going to be her husband. Brent knew that the intent of his stare would be enough to turn Boz around.

It did. Boz turned to see Brent, and he blinked. Brent watched as Boz said something to his friends, and all half-dozen or so turned in their direction. All of them were big construction workers, who could easily wield a jackhammer and their fists.

Brent felt someone take him by the shoulders, to try and turn him. Boz got up and headed in their direction. Two others from his table followed at a short distance.

Boz stood an easy six-four, the linebacker's body still on him even two years out of high school. "Whatchu starin' at, Bent?" he asked, calling him by the stupid nickname he had from high school.

"Hello, Craig," Brent said, keeping his voice low. He knew Boz hated being called by his first name.

"Thought you left."

"I went in the Army."

"Just get out?"

"Visiting."

"Uh-huh." He glanced back at the two men who stood a respectable distance away. "Still with the same crowd. George, Matt."

Said George, "Heard you're finally putting on the ball and chain."

"You would call it that," said Boz. "Some of us have grown up and know when we've got a good thing."

"Or you're pussy-whipped."

Matt snarled, "George, shut the fuck up."

Boz sneered. "Like you'd know how it is." He turned to Brent. "I'd know if I'd be pussy whipped, especially by the pussy I'll be getting."

Brent leaned forward and Matt stood in front of him. "Brent, no."

Brent held the cue stick. Like the staff, it could hold excess energy. Brent felt the fire in his belly and it was already in his arm, ready for casting. Brent stepped back, getting clear of Matt. He moved the stick in an arc in front of him.

"Going to come after me with that?" Boz said. "Old Man Black will never let you back in here."

Brent said, "She's not pussy."

Boz merely grinned. "Upset that she's not your pussy? Or going to defend her honor, Jarhead?"

Brent slammed the cue stick's fat end on the floor, making it jump up into his hand. He held it like he held the staff at casting — horizontally, the tip away from his body. The spell flew out from the tip, propelling the plastic and felt cap forward; at the same time sending Boz flying all the way across the room, through tables and chairs and into a bar stool, then the bar itself.

The bar had suddenly gone silent except for the noise from the TV's. The two bartenders looked in Brent's direction, seeing the smoking and exploded pool cue. Brent dropped the remnants of it and said, "I'm ready to go home now."

Said Matt, looking out at the destruction, "Good idea."

The bouncer didn't stop him because he didn't know if he did anything. Brent couldn't cast a "forget me" spell on the entire room, but he did on the bouncer, long enough for the group to leave. On the way home, he had to do some dancing around the subject to explain how he did what he did. Matt told George again to shut the fuck up. They dropped him off at the door to his house. None of them said goodbye.

As he expected, his mother was up and waiting. "You're home early," she said. "I thought I'd still be watching Johnny Carson."

"Mom, Johnny Carson's been gone for a while."

She stood up and stretched. "They're all the same to me. Did you have fun?"

"Not really."

"Why?"

"I got into a fight."

"Oh, Brent, with who?"

"Sarah's boyfriend. Who's now her fiancé, I guess."

"Honey," his mother came up to him. "I know that you really cared about her, maybe even loved her, but you've got to let her go."

"I know I do, it's just that…he dangled her in front of my face."

"Tell me you didn't hurt him."

I shot him with a pool cue. "I gave him a shove and walked out."

"You walked away, Brent."

He gave his mother a kiss. "I'm going to take a shower and go to bed."

"Sweet dreams."

THREE

He could see her, at the other end of the street. What was Sarah doing in this blasted-out village?

All he knew was he had to get to her.

He heard a child, off to his left. A baby, really, wrapped in a blanket. He could easily get it. But something felt wrong, off. He could envision a grenade under the swaddled baby — and because he could envision it, he knew it must be there. Everything he saw in his mind's eye was the truth.

He turned his attention to Sarah. All he had to do was run the gauntlet of buildings where there might be snipers or men with grenades.

"Help me!" she cried.

He had to save her, get her out of here, away from this place where she didn't belong, back home, to safety. She cried out for him.

He moved, staff extended. He noticed, about halfway to her, the baby wasn't crying any more. In fact, there was utter silence, except for his boots crunching on the sand and gravel, his breathing echoing around him. He tried to walk purposefully, heel to toe, to try and cut the noise. It didn't work.

Shooting erupted in front of him. Not at him but more like in front of—

"Sarah!" He summoned up his powerful shield and ran into the firefight. Bullets ricocheted off the shield as he dove from doorway to doorway, kicking in doors and raising the staff at shoulder level, ready to send a destructive force spell at anyone and anything inside.

No one was in any room. The gunfire came from all around him. One hit near his eye, causing his shield to ripple and his vision to go blurry. He plowed into one room, and saw the group of Taliban. Before they could grab their weapons, he threw them into the wall and one out the window. Sarah was screaming on the second floor. He looked up through the hole in the ceiling. He switched spells, dissolving the shield and flying up through the hole.

Sarah stood at the end of the other room upstairs, wearing a full *burqa*. Was it Sarah at all?

"I have a surprise for you," she said. She moved her hands under her robe and her hand darted out, along with a burst of fire. He didn't get the shield up in time.

The fire stuck to him, like gooey flames, and more came at him. His clothes went up like kindling. His skin caught next, the flying spell disappeared into tatters and he fell to the floor below.

He kept screaming, like he did when Torch did this to him in the magic school...the smell of his burning, crackling flesh...the noise of a helicopter, *whomp, whomp*, of the blades—

The barking of a dog.

The heat of a summer night.

A voice, "Brent?"

He struggled out of the village, his soul rising. He was dead meat, but his soul was everlasting.

"Brent. Can you hear me?"

He moaned. He opened his eyes. His father stood at the foot of the bed. The dog was standing up with his front paws on the bed, his hackles up. Brent had kicked off the covers, a heap at the foot of the bed.

"Yeah. Yeah." Brent rubbed his eyes.

"Pickles was barking," said his father.

"Sorry. Must've had a nightmare."

"I had to get up in half an hour anyway." He started out of the bedroom. "Join me for breakfast?"

"Out or in?" Brent felt like having a big, hearty breakfast. The only place he could think of was "Jake's? He said he'd give me a free breakfast."

"I wonder how that man stays in business. Gives away coffee to the homeless."

"Sometimes that's better to keep them quiet." Brent swung off the bed. "Let me get dressed."

Brent pet Pickles as his father left the room. Disturbing dreams were par for the course with magi, though this was the first time he had someone from home.

He got dressed and met his father, who was already working on a cup of coffee. His father drained the hot cup of coffee, something he had done for years and years. After taking care of Pickles, his father asked, "Ready?" Brent nodded. The two got in the car, and as his father drove down Edward Street, he said, "So. You hit Craig Boswell last night."

"I didn't hit him. I shoved him."

"Is that how he got a hole in his shoulder?"

"It was a pool cue tip."

His father sighed. "He's not pressing charges. Do you know what that means?"

"It means I'm off the hook?"

At a stoplight, Brent's father looked directly at him. "It means that you'd better watch your back, because he's going to take it in his own hands to come after you."

"I didn't touch him."

"But you used magic."

Brent looked out the window. "The things he was saying about Sarah, Dad…"

"Which shouldn't matter to you because she's not your girlfriend anymore." His father pulled into the parking lot, busy this time of morning. An hour before any major shift change, people would stop in for a quick bite before work if they had the time. "Better watch out with George."

"He was drinking a lot."

"He's been warned a few times for disorderly conduct. He's been doing drugs, too." That explained why George was "off". Was college life not appealing to him? Too much stress? Brent would have to catch up with him to find out.

His father got out of the car and led the way into the restaurant. "Hey, Mr. Rogers," called Jake Jr. He waved at Brent.

"Coffee?" asked the waitress as she walked by with two platters balanced in her hands. They both nodded, sat down at the nearest booth.

"Anything else I should know about my old high-school chums?"

His father sighed, putting four sugars in a tiny mug of coffee. "Two years is a long time, Brent. People change. I'm surprised you didn't outgrow them."

"Maybe I did. But they're still my friends."

The waitress poured the coffee as she set down the menus. Brent's father put his aside while Brent glanced at his. Too many choices this early in the morning. Brent shrugged and said, "Pancakes and bacon."

"Egg and cheese on English," said his father, handing the menu back. As the waitress left, his father said, "Oh, here." He pulled out his keys and started to thread out one of them. "Use this for the house until you leave."

"What are you going to do?"

"I never use it. Your mother's usually home by the time I get there. I'm on call this weekend, but next Saturday we can go to the beach with the kids." He drank his hot coffee. "Your mother wants a party on Sunday."

"Nothing big, I hope."

"Good God, no. Nothing like your send-off. Just the family."

Keithy, Lori, and of course, the grandkids. Loads of fun. "Great," Brent said, without any enthusiasm.

"Your mother wants any excuse to show off her cooking skills," said his father. "She's got some new appetizer recipes."

"What if I say no?"

"Not going to happen. Unstoppable force."

"Right." Brent drank his coffee. "What do you know about a Mark Pearson?"

"Doesn't ring a bell, why?"

"He was at the Red Bar yesterday."

His father smirked. "Checking up on me?"

"It was the only place I could think of to go and not worry about the rental."

He chuckled. "So what about him."

"He's thinking of suicide by drug-deal-gone-bad."

Brent's father took out a notebook. "Pearson?"

"Mark Pearson."

Their food arrived as his father scribbled in the notebook. "You talked to him?"

"It's what I got off him."

His father tucked the notebook away. "I'll ask discretely."

Brent dug into his pancakes, done perfectly. His father didn't eat a large breakfast. Said it slowed him down for the whole day.

They finished up together—the Army had taught Brent to eat fast. His father set aside the plate and the waitress came over. "On the house, boys," she said, smiled, and winked at Brent. Brent smiled back and waved to Jake.

His father drove him home. His mother was already gone, so he had the house to himself. Yesterday, he did a lot of driving. Today, he decided to take it easy. He parked himself on the couch, Pickles next to him, and he put on the TV.

He didn't notice he had dozed off until he heard the doorbell ring and Pickles bark in quick succession. *Oh, I am not going to sleep all day*, he thought, as he walked over to the front door. He checked the clock. He had fallen asleep for two hours.

He opened the door and his jaw dropped.

Even angry, Sarah Holdredge looked adorable. She came up to his shoulders. Her light blue eyes sparkled, her blond hair was cut in a layered frame around her round face. Her nose was rounded, her lips small but full. Her neck longer than normal, but delectable to touch…

"So you *are* back," she said.

He mentally shook himself out of his reverie. "Nice to see you, Sarah. Won't you come in?"

"This won't take me long. We can settle this out here." Her car was behind her, on the street. She jangled the load of keys in her hand, which were mostly key rings from different place she visited. He wondered if she still kept the ones he had bought her during their three years together.

"So, what's up?"

"You know what's up. You hit my fiancé."

"I didn't touch him."

"You shot at him! With...with..."

"Go ahead," he said, a smirk on his face.

"A pool cue," she said quietly.

"Do you know how preposterous that sounds?"

"You did it somehow," she said. "Some karate moves or something."

"I did not touch him," he said, adamant.

"Semantics. You pointed it at him and he went flying, and the pool cue hit his shoulder and went clean through it into the damn bar!"

"Do you believe that?" He laughed. "How could I do something like that?"

She put a hand on her hip. "Magic."

He raised an eyebrow. "Magic."

"Lori told me, so don't try to get out of it. She said you went to the Armed Forces Magic School."

He shrugged. "Do you believe that?" he said again.

"It doesn't matter whether I believe it or not. It matters that we've got witnesses that said you did it."

"Do you want to know what he called you?"

"What?"

"His pussy."

"Not any worse than some other things he's called me."

"And you stand for it?"

She glared at him. "Listen. It took me two years of therapy to get over you, you and your 'worship'. I wanted to be treated like a girl. A human being. Not some goddess that could do no wrong."

He stood there, silent. It was a repeat of when she broke up with him. "I want to be a person, not someone on a pedestal," she had said then. So, he treated every successive girl like a bimbo. And what did he get? Laid, yes. But loved, no.

"So Mr. Redneck Linebacker treats you the way you want to be treated?"

"He's there for me. He'll be there for me. He'll support me. Not like you who ran away to the Army."

"I don't consider going to war 'running away'."

"You didn't come home for over two years."

He smiled. She remembered!

"You enjoy it there, don't you?"

"What? *Enjoy* probably isn't the word I'd use."

"You want to go back there. You miss the adrenaline rush. I've read about people like you."

"Sarah, if you think I'm a risk-taker, you don't know me very well."

She took two steps down, her eyes at the middle of his chest. She had to look up at him. "All I know is you'd better stay away from my fiancé or we will get a restraining order against you. Or worse."

"He's not worth it. Not how he thinks of you."

"It's nobody's business but mine," she said. "Nobody's." Pickles followed her the three feet to the gate. She pet him before leaving.

He watched her get in the car and not look back. "What're you looking at?" he demanded of Pickles, who only gave him a happy dog grin.

★　　★　　★

"Whose car we taking?" Lori asked as she locked the door to her apartment.

"Mine," said Brent. "It has air-conditioning."

"Mine has air conditioning. You roll down the windows."

He smiled. They got into the rental. Lori was like a tourist, taking in all the bells and whistles and buttons. "Satellite radio?"

"Times, they are a-changing."

She crossed her arms. "Hey. Mine passed inspection last year."

Brent shook his head. "You can do better than that black bomber." He pulled onto the highway and they headed to the mall.

"Sarah came by," he said.

"What did she want? Not to get back together."

"I shoved her fiancé in a bar last night."

"Brent. She's so not worth it. Don't you think if she had half a brain she would have dumped that idiot by now?"

"Maybe she can't. He treats her like shit, and..." He thought, *What if she was being abused and she can't get out?*

"I think she likes the way he treats her. You know, you treated her like a queen and you got used for it."

He knew he was a clinging type, and when she did break up with him, he brushed the dirt from his shoes and vowed to not take her back, whatever she did. But if she showed up on his doorstep, though, he knew he couldn't say no. "We didn't go out to talk about this," he said.

"You brought her up."

"Forget I did."

She said nothing, played with her pony tail. He was able to see the outlet section near the mall and decided to go there instead of the mall proper. It was an open-air market/strip mall, with more places to go for protection or to hide and shoot from. He didn't have a focus, like a wand or a staff, but it wasn't necessary for magic to work.

He parked the car, looking around. Lori got out and Brent followed. He examined the area around him for hiding places. *A terrorist is not hiding in the mall, stop it.*

"We've got three hours," she said, thrusting her arm into his. She grinned. He pulled his arm away. "Oh, come on. Relax."

"Let's just get the stuff and leave, okay?"

"I don't come here that often. Why are you such a stick in the mud?"

Because the love of my life told me off after I hit her fiancé. "I'm having a bad day."

"Didn't want Wal-Mart?" asked Lori, as Brent ducked into Levi's. He walked in with purpose, to get a few shorts, some shirts. He would stop at Hanes for boxers.

"I want to impress my date."

"Brent, all you have to do is drop a few war stories about how you go after terrorists and I'm sure that'll impress her."

"It's not always that exciting." He made a bee-line to the jeans.

"Jeans? Why not Dockers?"

"I want to impress her, not intimidate her."

He picked out a few jeans and headed to the fitting rooms in back to try them on. Lori waited out in the store. When he came out, with the correct size pants on his shoulder, she was chatting up the cashier.

"Find what you need?" Lori asked, as he picked out two others the same size as the one on his shoulder.

"I'll go to American Eagle for the polos."

"Polos." Lori chuckled.

"I'm not wearing the t-shirts I had from high school."

"They got t-shirts here."

Brent sighed. The door opened and Brent turned to the door, seeing three gang-bangers enter the place. They didn't even look at Brent, but walked over to the leather jackets against the wall.

The cashier and Brent watched them warily. All three of them tried on the leather and denim jackets, easily the most expensive item in the store. One of them started walking to the front of the store with his on, and the cashier called, "Hey!" That's when they all bolted out the door.

Brent left his purchases and took off after them. He easily started to close the distance, because they didn't think anyone was after them, but when Brent got within two arm-lengths of them, they poured on the speed, knocking people aside as they ran.

Brent chose to keep pace with the one in the leather jacket, who started to fall behind his mates. Brent judged the distance and leapt, tackling the kid, skidding the kid's face into the concrete. The kid howled and the other two gang members paused a second, debated on coming back, but ended up taking off.

After Brent got up, he lifted the kid up by the collar of his jacket. He was thin and light, Brent noticed, and he had something in his hand.

Brent jerked back, his shirt getting sliced open by a switchblade. Brent hauled off and punched the kid solidly in the nose. He dropped the switch and his hands flew instinctively to his face. "Wha' the fuck, man!"

Brent felt someone grab him by the collar and yank him backwards off the kid. Brent let go, as the kid crumpled to the ground between two heavy-set men in dark blue security guard uniforms. Brent turned around to see another security guard holding him. "What's going on?"

"That kid stole that coat from the Levi's store."

"Fuck you, man! You jus' punched me for no reason!"

"We can solve this," said one of the heavy-set men. "Let's go." He pushed the thin kid toward Levi's. The security guard with Brent said, "You didn't have to punch him."

Brent pointed to the knife on the ground. The guard's eyes widened. "Oh, maybe you did." He bent down to pick it up.

"Use gloves," said Brent, knowing from experience about how to handle evidence—never put your fingerprints on the evidence. The guard paused. Brent covered himself by saying, "You don't know where that's been."

The guard pulled out some latex gloves from his pocket and picked up the switchblade. He used his shoulder radio to call it in, to have the Worcester cops come down and take Brent's statement.

Meanwhile, his sister came out of the store and saw him. Brent told Lori, "I'm going to make a report." He handed money to Lori and asked, "Buy the jeans, and get me two polos, one blue, one red."

The security guards brought him up to the security room, and the Worcester police arrived within ten minutes after the call. Brent gave his statement, the kid was arrested for shoplifting and assault with a weapon.

By the time he finished, he had an hour left. Lori was waiting for him outside of the security dispatch. "Are you okay?" she asked.

He took the bags from her. "I'm fine. The kid's in serious trouble, though." He peeked inside the bag. She had bought three polos, dark blue, green, and red.

"You have four pairs of jeans in there," she said. "The guy threw in a pair free for helping catch the kid."

He smiled. Maybe it wasn't going to be such a bad day after all.

★　　★　　★

After changing into the green polo ("It brings out the green in your eyes," said Lori) and a new pair of stonewashed jeans, he drove to pick up Chrissie. She waited outside the house next door to Keithy's, exactly like she said. Her hair was down and she wore a simple sundress with a thin shawl for an accent.

She got into the air-conditioned vehicle and sighed at the chill. "Hi," she said, smiling.

"Hi," he said. "You look nice."

"Thank you, so do you."

"So. How does Lucky's sound?" It was a general all-around "American food" joint with enough choices for everyone.

"Mmmhmmm."

"If you don't mind my asking, why so early?"

She looked out the window. "I have crowd anxiety."

Everyone had something wrong with them, it seemed. "So you avoid crowds?"

"When I can. I'm not good company at a baseball game. That's my deep, dark secret."

"If that's your deepest secret, we'll get along fine."

"You have crowd anxiety too?"

"I don't like them. Too much going on. Too much to keep track of."

She changed subjects. "So, Keith's your brother?"

"Yes."

"I feel bad for him. He said it all happened because of a car accident."

He hoped not to talk about Keithy. "Yeah," said Brent. "He got hit on the highway and pushed off to the median. It happened just when I passed my tests for the Army. He was fine."

"It scared him. I can understand that."

Brent snorted. "He wants people to pity him."

"He's got anxieties. Don't you?"

"Sure, I suppose. But mine are based on experience. I've seen people blow themselves up. I've seen terrorists shooting at people."

"So his fear is irrational."

"I think so."

"So's mine."

He glanced at her. She gave him a small smirk. A no-hard-feelings smile. He turned back to the road. "Can we talk about something other than my brother?"

"I was going to wait until you stopped driving before peppering you with questions."

"Thank you for that. So what about you?"

"Me. Well, I'm 24, I'm a Pisces."

He laughed. "I'm a Scorpio."

"Do you have any idea what that means?"

"No idea."

"They don't teach you that in Magic School?"

"I can't do astrology in the middle of a firefight." They pulled into Lucky's parking lot.

Lucky's looked like a storefront, since it was at the end of a small strip mall. It was still bright enough outside that they didn't have the lights on advertising the place.

They both walked into the well-lit restaurant, where the host greeted them, two menus in his hand. The place was empty at this hour. "Right this way." The music was mostly country, sounding a little like rockabilly, and was too loud for this empty place. However, as it would fill up, it would probably fade into the background noise of people talking to be heard over the music.

The host showed them to a wooden and leather half-round booth, big enough for them to stretch out in. A waitress came over soon after, introduced herself and asked what they were drinking. Brent played it safe and ordered a Bud; Chrissie ordered a margarita. "So, you're home visiting," Chrissie said.

"For a month."

"What do you think about the war?"

"To tell you the truth, I try not to think about it. It's a job."

"What do you do?"

"Heh. There's a lot of things I do. Man the sights to watch for snipers or ambushes."

"Did you ever get shot?"

"No."

"Your…platoon?"

"Team. Sure. But I'm a healer too, so they lived."

Their drinks arrived, but they hadn't looked at the menu. After some discussion, Brent called over the waitress and they ordered a general appetizer platter to start. Chrissie sat back when the waitress left, stirring the drink with her plastic stirrer.

"So you heal, too?"

"It's something we all have to learn in Magic School."

"What's it like? Like Harry Potter and you walk around in robes?"

He laughed. "Well, yes, in the school, you wear robes. It conducts the energy flow better when you're starting out. I found it easier in the field to wear a uniform with body armor."

"Army, right?"

"Or whatever branch you go into." He drank his beer. "Everyone's taught the same basic spells at first. After six months or so, depending on how good you are, you get specialty training. If they have someone who can teach you."

"What about you?"

"What *about* me?"

"Did they have someone teach you?"

"I can't talk about that. It's classified."

Chrissie continued with her questions, relentless as any reporter. "How many magicians are there?"

"Magi."

"Sorry."

"It's a common mistake. We get called all sorts of names. Wizard, Warlock, Magician…"

"What do you want to be called?"

"I like Wizard. Makes me think I'm older than my years."

"All you need is the beard."

"Against regs."

"So how many magi?"

He smiled. "Classified."

She huffed, though it wasn't meant to be angry. "So you killed people?"

"Once or twice."

"You said before, 'I try not to'."

"My brother was there. He'd want the gory details."

"So do I." At his look, she said seriously, "But not if it bothers you."

"Those are things I regret." He paused. "I don't want to bring that up."

The waitress returned during the silence, presenting them with the appetizer platter and plates. He was surprised that it had arrived so quickly. She also took their order for dinner. Chrissie chose a quarter pound burger with fries; Brent got seafood Alfredo, a special on the menu.

"I'm sorry," she finally said.

"What's with the twenty questions anyway?"

"It's fascinating to know someone who does magic."

He glanced at the food, taking a mozzarella stick. "I can't talk about most of it." He leaned on the table. "So what about you?"

"What about me?"

"Have you lived here all your life?"

"Since about a year ago. My family moved down to Florida and I stayed up in New England."

"New England over Florida? Are you kidding?"

She smiled a bit. "I have a brother. He's...he's not right in the head, as my dad says. He's manic-depressive. Really bad."

"Oh. I'm sorry."

She shrugged, ate a jalapeño.

"You don't like talking about yourself?"

"My life is so boring."

"Boring is good sometimes. Why don't you start at the beginning?"

"Well..." She grinned and said, "I was born on March 14, 1981 in Brighton, Mass, to Peter Armstrong..."

"So your last name is Armstrong."

"Christina Lynn Armstrong."

"Pretty name."

She smiled. "Thanks."

"Did you go to school in Brighton?"

"Yeah. I applied for Worcester Poly Tech, but my SATs weren't good enough."

"So where did you go to college?"

"I didn't bother. My parents put aside money for me to go, but they lost it all in the crash of '98."

"Where do you work?"

"I work part time at Wal-Mart."

Maybe he should have gone shopping there today. Maybe he would have seen her. "Do you like it?"

She shrugged, "It's not exactly what I want for a career. I'm applying for other things, like maybe opener or closer or manager."

"You don't want to go to college?"

"You make it sound like it's necessary for me to go to college." She plucked at another jalapeño at the same time he did. She let him have it.

"It's one reason I'm in the Army, to get the GI Bill."

"What are you going to go into?"

"Uh uh, this is all about you. I'm done answering the twenty questions about me."

She sat back, crossing her arms, but giving him a light grin. "I think you have five questions left."

"I've only been interrogating you for ten minutes."

"Is that what it is? An interrogation?"

"I'm joking. It might've fallen flat."

She laughed. "No, I'm teasing. Man, you need to relax."

He knew that. He drank down his beer. The waitress arrived and asked if he wanted another one. He shook his head. "Just water." He didn't want Chrissie to think he was a lush.

"So, um…do you have any pets?" he asked.

"Nope."

"Do you like dogs?"

"I like dogs, yeah." She took a mini-taco, sliding it on her plate.

He waited for her to ask the question "Do you have a dog?" but she played by his rules. She knew she was playing by the rules, because she wore that little smile on her face that made her look both cute and daring at the same time. Finally, he said, "I have a German Shepherd."

"I love big dogs," she said. "I like pit bulls. I know, call me crazy. One of my ex's had a pit bull that thought she was a lap dog."

He laughed, imagining a big dog like that climbing up on Chrissie's lap. She asked him, "Where are you staying, with your parents?"

"Yeah." He wondered about her exes, now that she had brought it up. But now wasn't the time or place to discuss it.

Their food came, and the conversation drifted to food. She liked Thai food, but there was no good place around. He resolved that he would find one before he left. She liked to go to Boston for food, and told him of the places there and what she'd had—all while eating a thick but boring burger.

They finished dinner, Chrissie eating most of hers, and Brent almost licking the plate. Dessert would be next, but neither wanted it. He didn't want to leave right now. However Chrissie, he started to notice, was hugging the booth nearest the wall. He glanced around. It was getting pretty crowded.

He signaled for the waitress, and when the leather folder came, he took it from her. He said to Chrissie, "I got this."

Chrissie frowned. He waited for her to argue. He flicked his fingers, and his credit card appeared in his hand. She put her purse away. "I'll get you next time," she said.

"There's going to be a next time?" he asked.

"I hope so. I had a really good time. Did you?"

"Yeah. Yeah, I did."

As soon as the bill was settled, Chrissie jumped up and threaded her way quickly to the door. Out in the parking lot, she stood taking in gulps of the night air. He waited for her panic attack to subside.

"Sorry," she said. "I had noticed when we were finished that we were crowded on all sides."

"Next time I'll ask them to keep people away."

"You don't have to do that."

"I want you to have an even better time next time."

She looked up at him and beamed. He smiled, leaned down, and kissed her, just a peck, not asking for anything more. She pulled away, not quickly, but shyly. "I don't put out on the first date," she said.

"I'm not asking for that."

"I'm sorry. I've gotten burned too many times and—"

"It's okay." He took her hands and squeezed.

"We can do this again sometime."

"Sure we can."

She smiled, and they started walking to the car.

After he dropped her off he realized, *I didn't think of Sarah once.*

FOUR

Brent couldn't take it anymore.

Abandoning his cart full of pansies and mums, he walked up to the Muslim couple. He didn't want to do this. Something was screaming at him not to. But he heard Custer repeat "Hearts and minds" over and over until Brent finally moved.

The Home Depot was devoid of helpers, stock-people, and customers this morning; the Muslim or Indian woman with the head scarf and her husband in colorful "man-jams" were trying to manhandle a small palm tree into their basket. Never mind that the pot was too big, so was the palm tree. It would never survive in the New England weather.

"Excuse me," Brent said, forcing a helpful smile, "Need help?"

"Oh, yes, sir," said the man, Indian by his accent.

"I would get one of those pallets. It'll be easier."

"Good idea," and he looked at the woman. Her hair was covered, the shawl long enough to cover her face if she needed to. She fetched the pallet at the unsaid command.

It was a lot easier, the two men getting the pot on the pallet. The screaming voice in his head had calmed down, telling Brent that they weren't a distraction; they were shopping like at the bazaars where they looked you over, assessing whether you would be easy to manipulate or one of those assholes who bulled you over with their American attitudes.

As the two Indians approached the cashier, Brent returned to his cart. To surprise his mother, he was going to plant the pansies and the mums under the window in the front of the house. Creeper roses would go up beside the garage in the back. Maybe along the back fence, after the small line of trees before the dog run, he could plant a small garden. But, right now, they needed flowers.

When he got home, a car was in the driveway and Pickles was barking maniacally. Someone came out from behind the porch.

"Hey George," said Brent, getting out of his car.

"Hey, dude."

"Wanna give me a hand?" He opened up the rental's trunk, exposing pallets of flowers.

George was in sweat-shorts, sandals and a ratty t-shirt. He looked like he had been drinking or was high, with his blue eyes shining like glass. George looked from the pallets to Brent in confusion.

"Never mind," Brent said, and took out the first pallet of mixed flowers. These were going out front.

"I was gonna see if you wanted to hang out. I guess you're busy."

"Hang out and do what?"

"I got a case of Bud in the trunk. It must be five in Afghanistan."

"It's not." It was 2100, but people didn't drink much out there.

"Oh, well."

"I'm not drinking at ten-thirty in the morning." Brent pushed by him to get the second pallet. George headed to his car's back seat. Brent heard the crack of a can popping open. Brent stopped, walked over to George.

"What?" asked George, standing with an open beer can in his hand.

"You're turning into your stepfather."

"Yeah, well maybe he was onto something."

"So you'll get your girlfriend knocked up—again?"

He shrugged. "She didn't put my name on the birth certificate, so I don't have a kid. No name, no kid, no child support, so I'm free!" He raised his arms in victory, sloshing the beer.

"You're an idiot," Brent said, going back to the pallets.

"What makes you so special, Army grunt?"

"Sergeant."

"What the fuck ever." George slopped beer again as he brought his arms down. "You think because you went in the Army that you're bigger and better than us? Your friends?"

"No, just you."

The beer can came flying at him and exploded about half a foot away from Brent, showering him and his pansies with beer. Shards of aluminum fell onto the asphalt.

Brent stood there, while George said, "The fuck?"

"Try that again and I'll send it back to you as if it weighed thirty pounds, and trust me, it'll go right through your head."

George looked at the shrapnel, back at Brent. "I see how it is." He walked around to his car. He backed out, barely missing Brent, and took off with a squeal going the wrong way down the street. Brent sighed, put the pallet of flowers down, and went into the house.

Pickles was overjoyed to see him. Brent headed into the cellar, found the old gardening tools. He didn't have a hoe, so it looked like he'd be on his hands and knees putting in the flowers. As long as he got it done by the time his mom got home.

He started planting the front first, getting down and dirty with Pickles. He dug up bones of a small animal, a hamster or a gerbil. Pickles dug up the thick, loamy soil that had often been used for flowers, until his mother started working full time. Brent laughed, pushing the dog out of the way as he planted.

He finished the front right side, had lunch with Pickles. He was getting started with the second pallet when the green bomber, Matt's car, pulled in.

"Hey," said Matt, going up to Brent. Brent was on his knees in the dirt, his hands coated with black loam.

"Hey, you."

"George come over?"

"Yeah."

"Was he drunk?"

"Something like that."

Matt sighed. "He's changed."

"Couldn't tell." Brent started putting in the second group of flowers. "So why?"

"School. Real life. He got kicked out of the house so it's not like he's doing it all of a sudden. He's just been doing it a lot more often."

"You want me to forgive him, excuse him, or what?"

"You're only here for a month. You're not going to change him between now and then."

Brent sat back on his ankles. "I'm not like that. Not anymore. I don't have the patience for that kind of shit anymore."

"The Army does that, I guess?"

"Did you come here to talk about him? To make amends for him?"

"Yes, on the former. Not necessarily on the latter."

"Then we're done with this conversation."

"He wants to get together on Friday." Matt stood there for a moment as Brent bent down to place another flower in the dirt.

"I might have plans." He was going to call Chrissie and see if she wanted to do a movie. Being that it was Friday, she probably didn't want to because of the crowds, but it wouldn't hurt to ask.

"Good," said Matt. "I hate to say it, but he's not that great to hang around with any more."

"Drunks usually aren't. Unless you're a drunk too."

"Then it's a blast." Matt kept a straight face. He wasn't amused. "I can't tell him to go fuck himself."

"You might have to. Look," Brent sat back again. "It happens all time in-country. You get one or two guys who are drunks. They get told, and they still do it, they send guys like me to deal with the hangovers."

"You? What do you do?"

"All of us wizards have a spell to get rid of hangovers. It's also used in torture." He bent to the flowers. "One guy said it felt like someone pulled his brains out by his ears."

"You know," said Matt, coming closer and standing directly over Brent, "You scared the shit out of me when you threw Boz across the room."

Brent patted the dirt. He could say he didn't mean to, but that would be a lie. He meant for the whole room to know he was not to be fucked with. So in answer to Matt, he only shrugged.

Matt took that he didn't care. "Oh, well, be seeing you around."

"Yep," said Brent, getting back to work.

What bothered Brent was not the possible loss of his friends. He was in a weird place his friends and family wouldn't understand. There was one person who might understand. Brent would go talk to him, probably tonight, since it shouldn't be busy. His father might understand, dealing with suspicious people all the time. But others? His friends? No.

He finished up the last bed of flowers, took a shower, and started dinner.

Anesthesiology was on the sixth floor, usually off-limits to patients. Brent knew his way around the hospital, so could find his way to the offices. He walked past the empty receptionist, down the short cubicle hall. He heard classical music coming from one of the cubes, so he headed in that direction.

He saw a man sitting back in his chair, hands entwined on the back of his head, atop his short salt-and-pepper hair. He sat relaxed, eyes closed. He was built compactly, like a drum barrel with thick sticks for legs and arms. In front of him, a computer played a concerto through two speakers on the desk.

"Brent," he said, his eyes still closed. He opened them slowly, and turned his chair around to look at Brent. His eyes were translucent grey. "Or should I say, Sergeant Rogers?"

"I'm not in uniform, Dr. Bates," said Brent. How did he know?

"So particular." He sat up straight, used his mouse to shut off the computer's music. He then turned to face Brent. "How's Army life?"

"Not as bad as I thought."

He grinned. "I told you. And the magicians?"

"Not bad."

"A man of ambiguous words," said Bates with a laugh. "I'm sure you didn't come here for small talk."

"My sister."

"Lori Rogers."

"Stay away from her."

Bates blinked. "I'm not even trying."

"The way she sounded—"

"Brent, you know me too well. If there is something I want, I get it." He stood, languid and graceful for such a compact man. "Would you like a coffee?"

"Not this late." Brent had been taught by the old vampire standing before him not to look him in the eye, so he kept his eyes down.

"I'm due." He checked his pager. "Going to be quiet unless Room 215 decides to drop the baby."

Brent knew he was trying to avoid the subject, so he brought it up again. "What about my sister?"

"I will avoid her or be very professional."

Brent wanted to tell him, *And don't feed from her.* Why, he wasn't sure himself. "Thanks."

"There's something I need of you."

"Me?"

"I don't know how you'll feel about it, being in the Army and all that, but I need a bodyguard/escort for a fundraiser on Saturday night."

"Escort?"

"More like 80% bodyguard, 20% escort."

"Don't you have people for that?"

"Of course I do. But since you're here…"

Why him? He could only think of one reason: someone was after Bates. "There's a hunter in town?"

"No," said Bates. "It's illegal to hunt in Massachusetts. I know what they teach you in the specialist school; I know how dangerous you are, just by standing before me. You do know a fire spell, yes?"

"That's not my specialty," said Brent. "But I do know one, yes."

"That's all I need. I know what abilities you have."

"How?"

"I have people for that." He smiled, incisors slightly longer than a human's but not quite like fangs. "I'll pick you up Saturday at seven."

"Is this a black tie event? It's not like I have a tux in the closet."

"Not everyone has a tux? Heathens. I'll send someone over with some evening attire tomorrow. Including shoes."

Brent said, "Yes, definitely the shoes." Brent started to walk out with Bates. "What's the fundraiser for?"

"Federal recognition of vampirism, ultimately."

"Seriously?"

"Right now, it's the legalization of privately owning bodily fluids for personal consumption."

"I'm sorry, that's —"

"Gross? We're trying to cover all bases, but I know it's gross."

The vampires had been talking about being legal for years. Since many "came out", some states, New England primarily among them, legalized their existence, so they were concentrated in New England. Bates had been an anesthesiologist in UMass, Mass General, and other smaller hospitals since the 1950's. No patient died under his watch. The blood never bothered Bates, and he never, ever fed from a patient. He would feed from willing staff, however. And one of his most willing was Brent during his time in UMass.

They got to the main lobby of the hospital. It was brightly lit, with a different security guard than before, and open even though it was after hours. Bates smiled, put a hand on Brent's shoulder. "I will see you on Saturday."

"Sure thing," Brent replied, stepping out from under the vampire's ice cold touch.

FIVE

★ *WORCESTER, THURSDAY* ★

The next morning his father was working on a cup of coffee when Brent got up. "George got arrested on a DUI," he said. That woke Brent up.

"How?"

"Ran onto someone's lawn. His parents won't post bail." He drank the coffee. "Don't you think about it."

"I wasn't going to."

"Maybe a night in jail will sober him up."

Or make him worse. He'd seen it happen in the Army. Some people, no matter how many hangover spells he would perform, would still go out the next night and find illegal hooch somewhere and drink themselves blind again.

"What are your plans for today?"

"I don't have any."

"Tony's been asking about you. I think he wants you to do tricks for his daughter's birthday party."

Brent sighed. "I'm not that kind of magician."

"I've told him that but he won't listen to me."

"I'll talk to him."

His father made a quick breakfast of eggs, toast, and hash browns in the toaster oven. After that, they went to the office. It was still early enough that not many people were there. There was a steaming hot cup of coffee on Tony's desk, but no Tony.

"He'll probably be right back," said Brent's father, leaving for his desk.

A half-second later, Tony wove his way between the desks, chairs, and filing cabinets to his desk. "Hey, Brent."

"Hey. You wanted to see me?"

"Yeah." He ducked into his desk drawer and pulled out a folder.

"Tony, I don't think I can—"

"It's one of *mine*."

Brent blinked. He had known Tony was an alpha male of a small pack for a couple of years now. When he accented the word, it meant this was a member of the pack.

"One of the Children did it?"

He shook his head. "One of the Destroyers."

The Children of the Moon, the vampires, werewolves and the like, had enemies among humankind, or even among their own kind. Called "Destroyers," these men or women could be everything from religious extremists to someone who was turned against their will. Brent had heard of the Destroyers through Dr. Bates, and in the Army. Both of them had told him to stay clear of the Destroyers because of their single-mindedness to eliminate every one of the Children they could find.

Brent sat down at the desk. "Don't tell my father."

Tony shook his head. He got out a legal pad and gel pen and set both in front of Brent. Then he walked away with his cup of coffee.

Brent opened the folder and concentrated on the first line, the name of the victim, Zak Aconte. He was discovered fully clothed, so he hadn't changed into a wolf or a wolf-man. He was shot in the head with a gun, but they recovered a silver arrow from his body. Whoever killed him knew he was a werewolf, a child of the moon.

Brent scribbled things. Where the arrows came from. Who made them. Where the murder took place and who had brought the body. There were three men, but only one man was clear in his mind, which meant the two others were probably dead. The one who was clear, though, didn't have a name, so he described him as best he could.

He stopped finally, breathing heavy. So much descriptive information poured onto the page that his hand cramped. Some words were written on top of each other, so he tried to transcribe them as best he could.

His father came over. "You didn't."

Brent looked up. "I had to."

His father took the folder from his hand, and Tony again appeared. Tony said, "Jim—"

"You know, he's not one of us, and he shouldn't be expected to do our work."

"This one's cold. Before he even got here."

"2000. You've been holding it for him?"

"No, I've been trying to get help with it for years. Personal."

Brent's father glared at him. "Next time, ask me."

Tony said, "What's the problem? Only you can use him because he's your own son?"

His father's brown eyes darkened even more. "That's the point, Tony. I don't want him being *used*."

Brent looked up at his father. "Dad, it's okay."

His father sighed. "I can see it now — you'll get whisked away to the FBI and have to work in some room somewhere where they hand you blank forms like this and force you to find out where Jimmy Hoffa is buried."

Said Tony, "Giants' stadium, don't you know that?"

"This isn't funny." He looked at Brent. "Does the Army know?"

"They think it's a spell, Dad."

"As long as they think they did it, not that you have the ability for it." He put a hand on Brent's shoulder. "I don't want you forced by the government to do something against your will."

"He's in the Army," said Tony. "They beat you to it."

He saw the veteran from Desert Storm setting up a table outside of Wal-Mart. He wore western "desert camo" shorts, which exposed his prosthetic leg.

Brent helped with the table. "Hey, thanks, man," said the guy.

"No problem, sir."

The man smiled. "Navy?"

"Army, sir."

"Me too. 101st Airborne."

"Don't know any of them."

"What division are you in?"

"Magician's Corps."

The man chuckled. "I'm way before your time, son."

"Desert Storm?"

The man nodded. "Captain Dan Lynch." He held out his hand.

"Sergeant Brent Rogers." He almost saluted, then shook the man's hand.

"Take a seat 'til my partner comes."

"It won't seem right."

"Then stand there and look ominous."

Brent sat down.

Dan talked of war before the Magic Corps. The reliance at the time was on technology, unmanned drones with cameras, robots and men in tanks and on the ground. Higher casualty rates, more loss of limbs, more fog of war. Now, with the Magic Corps, the magicians with their higher senses and longer range, could see through the fog of war or heal a man so he could have the better quality of life he could expect if he had all four limbs.

"Who are you?" demanded a short man in a Green Beret cap, glaring at Brent.

"Bernie," said Dan, getting up. "Take it easy."

"It's all right. I'm just leaving."

Said Bernie to Dan, "None of your friends get to sit around with you, I told you that already."

"Bernie, he's in the Army. He's one of ours."

Bernie looked him up and down. "Join the VFW. We don't want the likes of you here."

"I'm just leaving," Brent said again, standing. He looked at Dan, then looked at Bernie. He looked up at the sky. "Looks like rain."

"What?" Bernie said, looking up. "I don't see no—"

The rain exploded from a cloudless sky. Brent dusted his hands and walked into the store.

The rainstorm was located only in front of Wal-Mart's exit, so people were smart and used the entrance, avoiding the table. Brent knew that what he was causing was a total paradox. Paradox happened when people saw magic that they didn't think was possible, and they use their rational minds to explain it. Or they ignore it, or their minds break trying to explain it. He luckily had not seen the last happen in the field, because all soldiers were now exposed to magic in some way.

When he came out, he also used the entrance door, but passed by the table and put money in the jar. Dan got up, while Bernie looked away. He walked with Brent out of the rain, and out of earshot of Bernie. "Look, I'm sorry about Bernie."

Brent looked up at the sky above them. "You want me to stop it?"

"If it's not too much trouble."

"I'm sorry, sometimes my temper gets the better of me." He looked up again at the rain. It slowed to a drizzle, then mist, then stopped.

"That's why you never existed in Desert Storm." Dan gave a sketchy salute and went back to the table.

"Uncle Brent!"

Brent groaned. Pickles barked. Lori let the three rugrats loose in the house.

Two piled on him on the couch. Dante almost got him in the groin. Kaitlyn smothered him with kisses, and Ashlyn shuffled in, standing near the TV.

"If I didn't know better," said Lori. "I would think you didn't want to see them."

"Whatever gave you—" he grunted when Dante punched him. Brent grabbed Dante's hands. Dante yelled and kicked Brent in the shin.

The sleep spell was on the tip of his mind, and he would have completed it if Kaitlyn hadn't thrown her arms around him, hugging him fiercely. He pushed her away.

Ashlyn, six, stood at a distance with her fist in her mouth. She gazed at him as if he was something she'd never seen before. Lori carried a backpack into the kitchen. Dante screamed, "Ice cream!"

"I'll see if Gramma has any," said Lori.

Dante was the youngest at three and born a week before Brent left for the Army. Of much darker coloring than the blond, blue-eyed girls, no one knew who Dante's father was, and Lori had put "unknown" on the birth certificate.

Dante took a running leap at Brent. Brent held up a hand in a certain position and the boy slammed into the force field Brent created. *Maybe it can stop a train*, he thought, as the boy bounced off it onto his ass.

Brent could see a mixture of emotions play out on the boy's face. He was shocked, angry, and then he started to cry.

"What did you do, Brent?" Lori demanded, coming out of the kitchen with an ice cream cone.

Kaitlyn pouted, "Can I have an ice cream cone?"

Lori unwrapped the cone for Dante saying, "Go get one."

Ashlyn stood in the middle of the floor, fist lodged further in her mouth.

Lori waved the ice cream cone and Dante jumped up, anger and fury gone. He almost tackled his mother for the treat. Brent stared at Ashlyn. "What's wrong with her?"

Lori shrugged and said to her, "Get that out of your mouth."

Ashlyn blinked like a slow-moving ox at her mother. After Dante threw the wrappings of the cone on the floor, he took Brent's place on the couch. Lori absently pulled Ashlyn's hand out of her mouth.

Brent wanted to go to his room and lock the door to escape the chaos. When he had left, they were babies. Kaitlyn had only recently been potty-trained before he left, Ashlyn was in diapers,

Lori was going to court to get her ex-husband to pay child support for the two girls.

Kaitlyn came up to him again, an ice cream cone in each hand. "Want one?"

"No, thanks," he said. He noticed she was wearing bright red nail polish. *Already?* He thought. *She can't be into that whole makeup thing already.* He moved into the kitchen, as Pickles stood at the couch, expectantly waiting for an opportunity to pick up any ice cream droppings.

Lori swept her hair back after throwing out the paper. "You don't mind watching them 'til Mom gets home, do you?" she asked.

He found that he would rather go up one of the mountains in Afghanistan in full kit under enemy mortar fire than watch her kids. "I do mind," he said.

"Oh, come on. They love you."

Ashlyn had moved from the middle of the floor to the edge of the couch, fist back in her mouth, eyes wide at the TV. Dante laughed uproariously and loud at something. Kaitlyn sighed dramatically.

Brent was more concerned with Ashlyn. "Is she okay?"

Lori walked over to the door. "Tell Mom I'll pick them up later. Bye!"

"Lori!" but she slammed the door behind her. What was she doing? He started to the door to follow her. "Don't you have to work?" he yelled out the door at her.

She was in her car, and reached over to yell at him through the open passenger-side window. "Not tonight!" She waved at him.

"What about Alan?" They were his kids. He was her ex-husband. "Can't he watch them?"

"Not his night!" She backed the car out of the driveway. Brent stood in the doorway of the foyer, wondering what had just happened. He headed back inside.

Kaitlyn walked to the kitchen table, carrying her backpack. Dante was settled on the couch smearing ice cream all over it. Ashlyn stood at the corner of the couch, away from her brother. She looked up and stared at Brent, her blue eyes wide and afraid. He'd seen that look on kids in the mountains. He didn't make any threatening moves, but he smiled at her and said, "Hi."

She stuck her fist in her mouth and ran to her sister. She put her arm around Kaitlyn. Kaitlyn hugged her and said, "It's okay, it's Uncle Brent. He won't hurt you. Here, want to color?" Kaitlyn pulled out a coloring book and a box of crayons from her backpack. Ashlyn gathered the items and sat down on the floor to color. Kaitlyn smiled at Brent and ate her ice cream cone.

All was calm again, though Brent didn't know what to do with himself. He looked from Kaitlyn to Ashley to Dante. Kaitlyn said, "Want to play a game?"

"Sure," Brent said, focusing on that, because he felt that a tornado had gone through the room.

Kaitlyn pulled out a paper and pen and set up a tic-tac-toe board. Brent sat down and played a few rounds of that with her. She was smart, setting up the board so she could win. Brent asked, "Do you know how to play cards?"

"Go Fish," she said.

"I know there's cards around here somewhere." Brent got up to look in the junk drawer in the kitchen.

Dante jumped off the couch and ran into the kitchen, "Cookie!" he demanded, pointing vaguely at the kitchen cabinet. Brent looked in that direction and said, "No, you're going to get supper soon." At least, that's what his mother used to tell him when he tried it.

However, when he was Dante's age — maybe — he would skulk away. Not throw himself on the floor and scream, beating his head and fists against the linoleum.

Holy shit, what the hell happened? Did Lori screw the devil himself for this child? He was a baby before. Sure he cried a lot, but he never pulled this shit.

He looked helplessly at Kaitlyn, who watched her brother and shook her head. Sighing, she said, "Let him scream."

He guessed that was what Lori did, so he turned back to looking in the kitchen drawer for the deck of cards. Ashlyn was still sitting on the floor, watching the whole exchange with a bemused look on her face, as if she were watching him on TV. The screams got louder, the banging got harder. Brent was afraid he was going to hurt himself.

Then Dante slowed down. Brent turned his back on the boy, back to the drawer. He found the cards in the back at the same time he heard a girl's scream behind him. Kaitlyn yelled at Dante, "Stop that!" at the same time Ashlyn screamed, and he turned around to see Dante moving his face away from Ashlyn's arm. Ashlyn was crying, holding her arm.

"Did he bite her?" he asked, bending down to Ashlyn. She backed away from him, so Kaitlyn ran over to her. Kaitlyn said, "Yeah," checking over her sister's arm.

Brent glared at Dante, who stood up and yelled, "Cookie!"

"Oh, you think so?" Brent pointed to the couch. "Get in there!"

"COOKIE!"

Brent could feel his control slipping. He was ready to whip out a push spell and shove the kid into the other room so hard that he would bounce off the wall like a tennis ball. He raised his hand, getting ready to hit him with the spell, when he heard a car come into the yard.

He walked to the foyer and looked out the window to see his mother's car. He turned slowly to see Dante pushing the chair against the counter, with the obvious intention to climb up it.

"You're so lucky," Brent said, and walked over to him. He grabbed Dante's arm and whipped him away from the chair. Brent bent down so he was eye-to-eye with the boy. 'NO."

The kid moved his head forward, as if to bite him. Brent jerked back and barely stopped himself from slapping the child in the face. Kaitlyn yelled, "Gramma!" as he brought his arm down.

He looked at his mother, and he knew his fury was right there in his eyes, because his mother, after briefly hugging Kaitlyn, rushed over to Brent and Dante. She stood between the two as Brent stood up to his full height, ready to stare the kid down.

"Cookie!' Dante cried.

His mother got the cookie.

Dinner was another strange affair. His father worked late — or he was warned, Brent thought sourly — as his mother made three different meals. Ashlyn ate only French fries and chicken strips, Dante ate French fries and plain spaghetti, and the rest of the family got spaghetti with meat sauce. Dante threw fries at Kaitlyn, who took her plate to the living room to eat. Dante almost threw food at Brent, but he gave him a look of death while he held the nugget in his hand. Instead, he ate it, grinning maniacally.

At midnight, Lori crawled in, smelling of smoke and beer. She arrived in a mini-skirt and sequined halter top, heels as long as her feet, and heavy running make-up. Brent had to do a double take. This was his *sister?*

"You dropped them off so you could party?" Brent slowly rose from the couch where his mother jerked awake from a doze.

"You can't bring a kid into a bar, Brent."

"You could have told me you were going out."

"Why? Are you the boss of me?"

His mother said tiredly, "Both of you, stop it."

"I knew you'd think that way, Brent."

"You have a job. And kids."

"I work part time and Mom doesn't mind watching the kids, right?" Lori looked at her mother, who looked ready to drop where she stood. Lori got the kids going and hustled them out the door before Brent could say another word. His mother bent to pick up the toys, but Brent said, "I got this."

Gratefully, she went to bed. As soon as the door closed, he stood in the center of the chaos. Toys, crayons, books, more toys, broken toys, broken crayons littered the floor, the couch, the kitchen table. Brent closed his eyes, sensing where everything should go. When he opened them, he was in the center of a maelstrom of flying toys that all flew into their respective bins.

The magic was set free, and he loved the feeling. Although it was powerful, he restrained it to his bidding by his will. This is what he missed most. In the field, he could let loose — to hurt, to heal, to be the wizard.

He sensed rather than saw the room was clean. He reigned in the power, keeping it to himself, and opened his eyes. Not a speck of dust was out of place. He couldn't help it; he grinned.

SIX

Chrissie was out of breath when she answered the phone. "You okay?" Brent asked.

"Was in the other room," she said.

"Oh. It's only me."

"I know. What's up?"

"I was wondering if you'd like to go out tonight."

"Oh, I can't. I always work weekends."

"What if you didn't have to work."

"I need the money," she said. "I'm only part time, so any hours I get are great."

"Because I can help you get the night off."

There was a knock on Brent's door. Chrissie laughed in the phone and said, "No, Mr. Magic Man. I need the cash."

"Hold on a sec." Brent walked over to the door. A big bald man stood there, dressed in business casual, holding a set of clothes on a hanger and a pair of shoes in his other hand. "Sergeant Rogers?"

"Yes?"

"From Dr. Bates."

"Thanks." Brent took the clothes that were in in a dry-cleaning plastic bag, along with a pair of shoes. He saw the shoes were Army-issued shiny leather. Then he lifted the bag to look at the clothes.

They were his dress greens, pressed neatly. He looked up at the man. "How?"

The man shrugged. Chrissie was calling his name.

"Better take that, Sergeant," said the man as he left.

Brent put the phone in the crook of his neck. "Sorry, had a delivery."

"Oh," said Chrissie. "Is it something good?"

"My dress uniform." With every patch and medal from the Corps. Team patches were mostly meant for his working uniform back in Afghanistan.

"What? Why?"

"I have a formal function to go to tomorrow."

"Oh. That's good, right?"

"If I'm in my dress greens, it's more formal than I thought."

"I'd better let you go," she said. "Sorry about tonight."

"No, it's okay. Maybe…Monday night?"

"Yeah. Yeah, Monday night, if they don't call me in."

"They won't."

She laughed. "Don't you dare, Magic Man. I'll talk to you soon."

"See you later." He hung up, looked at his uniform. Who the hell got his shit out of his kit without his protection spell going off? He opened the plastic and examined the uniform more closely. It had his marksman medal that he got at boot, his Corps medals for offensive magic and the mage red cross for healing.

"Well, Pickles," said Brent, hanging up the uniform, "What do you do on a Friday night?"

Pickles grinned.

"Go find some lady dogs? Just might. Be my wing man?" He laughed, hugged the dog.

A couple of hours later, he was on the road when his text notification tone sounded. He pulled over into a parking lot and checked. He had seen the "Don't text and drive" signs and took them to heart.

"What u doin 2nite?" Keithy's phone number showed up next to the text.

"Nothing, y?"

"Party @ my house 6"

Why not. "OK"

"Cya."

He supposed he owed Keithy an apology, after all.

Keithy seemed to like pop music, as Brent could hear it a block away. He parked around the corner and walked to the apartment.

Young women wearing halter tops, bathing suits, or other lack of clothing sat on the porch on the second floor, laughing, drinking, hanging out. They whistled when they saw Brent heading to the back door.

People crowded the stairwell—the party extended to the first floor, it seemed. Some grinning black man handed him a bottle. He passed it off to the next person without drinking from it. He pressed his way into Keithy's house.

"Hey," said an Asian woman, coming up to him. It was one of the women from the balcony. She was small with short hair, soft brown eyes that were wide from drugs.

"Hey."

She looked him over. "Do I know you?"

"No, I don't think so."

"You look familiar."

"I'm Keithy's brother."

"That might be it." She sipped a beer. "Do you want a beer?"

"Sure."

She waded into the crowd. He watched her carefully, as she walked over to the kitchen and pulled a beer from a tub of ice near the kitchen doorway. Someone clapped Brent's shoulder, making him duck instantly, turn around and almost grab someone by the throat.

The black man gasped. "Hey, man! Easy!"

Brent brought his hand down. "Sorry, man."

"Shit, calm down." The man smiled at Brent.

"Habit. What are you doing here, Ty?" Tybalt Johnson was one of the quarterbacks on the football team, not as spectacular as the other quarterback who happened to be friends with Boz. Ty never fit in to the football culture. He didn't lift weights and didn't look like he worked out much, though he did run to keep himself trim in high school. He had a runner's body, thin and lanky.

The Asian girl returned with the beer and Brent absently took it from her. "What're you," said Ty, "a cop or something?"

"Army." He drank the beer. In the hot apartment, it was very cold and nice going down.

"Oh yeah? Did a year in the Marines before my fuckin' knee gave out."

"Couldn't get a scholarship? First black quarterback in town."

He snorted. "Too slow, too skinny, too black for a QB. Football QB is a white man's game."

Brent drank. "Sorry to hear that, man." He looked around for the girl. She had wandered off.

"So you in Special Forces?" asked Ty.

"You could say that," said Brent.

"So secret that even you don't know?"

Brent laughed. "Not even. No, I'm in the Magic Corps."

"No way."

Brent nodded.

"The Marines said that the Wizards were all a bunch of pussies and queers."

"That's the Marines for you," said Brent. "I know that the Marines don't like the magi much. Marines would rather do things the old-fashioned way—with brute force." Brent had never worked with a team of Marines, but had heard stories about how they treated the wizards, until they were needed, of course. Brent took a whiff of the air.

So did Ty. "Shit," Ty said, "who's starting up the weed?"

Brent didn't want to go home smelling like pot. "I'm outta here if that shit's going down."

"Me too, man. I'll get you another beer, we'll go someplace quiet."

"Sure, man."

Ty pushed through the crowd to the kitchen and disappeared for a moment. Brent found his way to the door and stairwell where he could breathe. Ty appeared behind him with the two beers. He motioned upward with one of the bottles. They headed to the third floor, where it was hotter but without people. They sat on the step outside the third floor apartment. "These tenants won't mind?"

"They're probably downstairs." Ty took a pull on the beer. "What do you do in the Magic Corps?"

"I blow shit up."

Ty and Brent both laughed. "No shit?"

"No shit. I look for IED's, find snipers and enemies, point them out to the team for them to take them out. I blow up bombs at a distance. I can throw people and shit in the air with just a thought." He pointed to his head. "I'm not like other magi. They have to say the spell or wiggle their fingers."

"You think it and it happens?"

"Yup. It's why I'm a sergeant at 22."

Ty whistled. "That's awesome man. You're like a telepath."

"Telekinetic. Kinda." He drank, realized he almost drained the second bottle already. "You want me to show you a trick?"

"I thought you weren't a telepath?" Ty smiled in the dim light.

"Naw, it's what everyone wants to see once I tell them what I can do."

"Dude, if you blow shit up, I don't need to see that."

Ty drank from his beer while Brent laughed. "I know other tricks, simple tricks. But yeah, they mostly have to do with blowing shit up." Brent drained his beer and got up. "Want another one?"

"Nah, had my six pack limit. The party's gonna get stoned and stupid now."

"This party happens often?"

"Every weekend. Hey, give me your number. We can go get a coffee."

Brent gave Ty his number and followed him downstairs. "I need to see Keithy, at least show him I'm here."

"Okay, man, but if the cops stop you on the street, you're gonna smell like weed."

"I'll take my chances."

Brent walked into the second floor apartment. Someone had put on some loud rap music. He found Keithy in the living room, watching TV with the sound off, a few young people passing joints around. The Asian girl he had seen when he walked in sat on the couch near Keithy.

"Hey, Brent," said Keithy, his eyes glassy. "Glad you could make it. Want a beer?"

"Already had a couple."

"A hit?" Someone offered him a joint.

He passed it the person next to him. "No, thanks. I'm heading out."

"Heading out?" Keithy asked. "You just got here."

Brent glanced at the Asian girl. Keithy looked at her and smiled, then nodded to Brent. "Meet Kim. Kim, this is my brother, Brent."

Kim smiled and rose from the couch. She presented a limp hand for a handshake, as if she expected him to kiss it. He shook her hand. She was too thin, too cute for his tastes. She had a touch of white powder on her nose.

"Yeah. You know how Mom gets if I don't get home by a certain time."

Keithy laughed loud. "She sends Dad and the precinct after you!" He laughed again, and Brent uncomfortably started to back out. He knew this was his brother before the accident; fun-loving, carefree. Laughed at jokes and played pranks. But this was his brother before, on steroids. Laughing too loud, too free.

Kim was waiting for Brent to make a move, but Brent only nodded to her. "Excuse me," he said.

"Come back soon!" Keithy yelled after him. "I'll show them the pictures of you in the tub!"

Brent bent his head and almost bull-rushed his way out.

SEVEN

"Mom…"

She brushed off imaginary dust from his shoulders one last time. "There," she said, and stepped back again. She looked Brent over with a smile tinged with tears.

"Geez, Mom, I'm only going to a party."

"It's a fancy party or you wouldn't have to dress up." He knew that, but didn't want his mother to worry. He was already warm in the air-conditioned room.

A horn beeped outside. He gave his mom a quick kiss. "Have fun!" called his father from the living room.

Bodyguarding, he thought. Right. He knew what he was.

Bates' meal.

He had done it often enough, as he worked at the hospital late at night, when transport and triage were slow. Bates would take him into one of the comfortable conference rooms with a couch. Then Bates would show his true colors. He and Bates had been lovers for three months before Brent went into the Army. While Bates would let Brent screw him, Brent would let Bates feed from him. Both actions were ecstatic to Brent.

The chauffeur stood outside the rear door of the car, his hand on the door handle. Brent nodded to him and the man nodded back, opening the door. Brent climbed into the Cadillac.

It smelled lightly of roses. Bates sat at the opposite door. "You look smart," he said.

"You're not so bad looking in a tux yourself."

"You flatter me."

The door closed as Brent laughed at the banter. It was like old times. "Have you…"

Bates nodded toward the tinted glass partition which separated him from the driver. "Part of my stable." Brent knew that was what some of the older vampires called people they fed from often. Newer vampires called them "tenants."

"Was I ever part of your stable?"

"No, because you never worked for me. It wasn't expected." He reached over and put a hand on Brent's knee. "You were pleasant."

"A diversion?"

"If you were a diversion, I never would have told you go into Magic Corps."

Brent paused, looked down at the hand on his knee. Bates didn't remove it. Brent didn't want him to. "Did you pull strings to get me there?"

"I only opened the door. You stepped through on your own merit, Master Sergeant."

"I wasn't as good as some of the others there, you know."

"How so?"

"I couldn't memorize the spells right. And when we had final exams, I went up against my old roommate from boot."

Bates rubbed his hand around Brent's knee. "You hesitated?"

"No. He was better than me."

"What did he do?"

"His phosphorous fire got through my shield and burned the hair off my face." It took months for his eyelashes to grow back.

"You have more than shield magic, especially when you have the ability for telekinetics and psychometry."

"Archmage Armond was the only one who knew about my knack."

"Why?" Bates sat up. "Why didn't you tell them?"

"My father told me to keep it under wraps." He knew why now. But as Tony had said, it was too late. He was a 22-year-old master sergeant in the Army, after all, one of the youngest at that grade and level.

"You should tell them. They may even make you archmage."

Brent shrugged, watched as Bates' hand moved to the inside of his thigh. His body reacted like he knew it would. "Doc, these pants aren't made for hard-ons."

Bates chuckled, pulled his hand away. "I can take care of it."

Brent turned to him. "I know you can."

Bates leaned over and gave him an open-mouthed kiss. Brent responded—it had been almost a four months since he had any sexual relations with a man. Bates' hands fluttered along Brent's tunic, fingers brushing over the medals. Bates pulled back, leaving Brent breathless and painfully hard.

Bates squeezed Brent's knee. "I promise, later. Did you remember to bring a sidearm?"

"Will I need it?"

"Hopefully not. But it's all in the impression you make." Bates turned to a compartment next to the fridge and opened it. He pulled out a gun and a shoulder holster, started altering the holster to a shorter height. "Needles won't mind if we borrow his."

Brent took the gun, taking out the magazine and checking the chamber. It wasn't loaded. It was a 9 mm, small in comparison to the Desert Eagle he had seen some of the men carry. It had a 10 round magazine, and an extra one in the pouch next to the holster. He hadn't worn a shoulder holster since boot. He didn't like them. They were uncomfortable and, for him, hard to reach.

As he shrugged back into his jacket after adjustments were made, Bates smiled.

"Will there be other vamps there?" asked Brent.

"Other kin, yes. Most are young and inexperienced. This will be a perfect time and place for them to see and be seen."

"Is that why you're going?"

"I am going to see the American Queen."

Brent blinked. "You said this was a fundraiser."

"Yes, that's the overview. Yet she is still going to be there. Most of the older 'vamps' are there to ask for boons."

"Is that what you're going for?"

"In a sense. But I'm actually going to provide her with a boon of my own." He smiled. "She will not be happy with that."

"What am I going to do, stop her from doing something?"

"Indeed."

He wondered if he could raise the force field fast enough against a queen of vampires. They were superhumanly fast, strong, and intelligent; perfect predators, excellent attackers. This was why there were so many of them in Special Forces.

"Are you going to introduce me as a Magic Corps sergeant?"

"Of course," he said. "I believe in giving my enemies enough information to hang themselves with."

"Ever been in war, doc?"

He grinned. "Oh, yes."

Brent laughed.

The car came off the road onto gravel. Brent rolled down the window and looked out into the night. He heard the cicadas, smelled the deep night jasmine.

"We still in Massachusetts?"

"New Hampshire," said Bates, looking at himself in a mirror.

The driveway opened up and they slowed down. Brent put up the window, trying to show patience. Bates, however, took down the dark glass partition separating them from the driver. Brent thanked him silently. He wanted to see the battlefield for himself.

It was a mansion, done up in old Victorian style, with gables and rooms that were not squared off. The limos and cars lined up at the front door, depositing their occupants. Servants in tuxes opened the doors for the visitors and guests. At their turn, the door opened on Brent's side.

Brent stepped out, feeling the tug of the gun as he did. He pulled down his jacket as Bates stepped out gracefully. He looked up at the building. "Good," Bates said.

"What?"

"I'm familiar with the layout of this house. In case we have to make a hasty escape."

Brent wondered whether he was protecting Bates for a good reason or a bad one.

Bates led them up the stairs into the foyer of the mansion. Keeping close to him, Brent kept his Army poker face on when he really wanted to gape.

As they walked through the ten-foot tall mahogany and gold doors, there was a deep foyer that led into an area with a set of double staircases and a chandelier. This room was crowded with people in various tuxes and evening gowns, talking among themselves in small huddled groups. Unless he touched them, he wouldn't know whether they were human or not.

Bates was stopped by a man with tousled brown hair. He looked out of place, like he belonged in a modeling studio, not here, despite the tux. "Dr. Bates," he said.

"Charles. Charles, please meet my companion, Master Sergeant Brent Rogers from the US Army. He's from Afghanistan."

Charles nodded once to Brent, who returned it, but not fast enough because Charles immediately returned his attention to Bates. "Mr. Phillips will be surprised to know you're here."

"I'm sure," said Bates. "You will, of course, convey my regrets that I don't give him my regards."

"I can find him for you."

"No need." Charles then violated the first rule of dealing with a vampire. Never look them in the eye.

Vampires were pure predators, like the cobra, and their eyes held not the mirror of their soul, but the power of their blood. This power could easily tame the wildest human, merely by an intent gaze. Looking into a vampire's gray eyes gave them power over a man, sometimes very limited, sometimes totally devoted. Brent and Bates had looked into each other's eyes before. Brent could trust Bates not to abuse that ability with him. He assumed Charles had done it with others and forgot himself when he looked into Bates' eyes.

Charles bowed and scraped. "Of course, sir." He backed off and away.

Bates turned to Brent. "We need to—"

"Doctor Bates!"

Brent held a hand up, ready to push the approaching man as he pressed in closer. The man stopped, beyond Brent's arm reach. However, Brent could easily give the man a shove with his mind, if necessary.

"I don't have time for this," said Bates. "Head to the ballroom," he pointed to a set of white French doors, where two men stood guarding and the other people seemed to stay away from them.

Brent said, "Excuse me," to the man, and pushed by him.

Some people called for Bates as they moved through the crowd; Brent sent gentle pushes to get people out of the way, heading directly to the door. They got through the foyer to the ballroom. At the doors, the two men nodded to them, and opened the door for them.

It opened into a large room, lit mostly with candles so the light was diffused. The floor was marble, the walls were marble, the ceiling looked like white marble. They walked into the room, and the door shut behind them. Some people turned to see the two men enter, but none approached.

"Against the wall," whispered Bates in Brent's ear, "are most of the young vampires. Their minions are in the ballroom, entertaining them by doing their little minuets."

But there was no music, no dancing, only people gathered in knots similarly in the other room. Brent looked at Bates, confused. "Their messengers were in the other room," he continued, as he plucked a champagne flute from a silver tray that a waiter brought by him. His nostrils flared, and he sipped the dark liquid.

"I don't get the dancing part."

Bates laughed. "These are the minions who are closest to their masters, and they are playing political games. We left the pawns; now we are among the knights, bishops, and rooks. Maybe one or two queens, as well."

Brent scanned the room. He could instantly tell the predators from the prey—the humans on display or doing their masters' bidding in the center of the ballroom floor, and their masters, watching like impassive statues along the wall. At the end of the room where the orchestra usually sat, a row of men stood facing out into the crowd. It wouldn't have been surprising if that was where the queen held her court.

"It seems we must approach the queen openly," said Bates. He glanced at either side of him, looking through the crowds to the walls. "Ready to run the gauntlet?"

"Don't stop?" Brent took his place in front of Bates.

"I will stop if necessary. Do not push, not even with your mind. The predators will find that offensive."

Brent and Bates started weaving in between the groups of people. Some assessed him with a smile, others with a frown, as if he didn't belong.

A man, too big to be human, stepped between a group of people and into their path. People split away, and Bates put a hand on Brent's shoulder.

"Arthur," said the man. His black hair was long, pulled back in a ponytail. His eyes were gray like the rest of the predators, translucent and dead. He was clean-shaven and built like a small-time gangster—all torso and thick, burly arms stuffed in a suit.

"Peter."

"Petrus."

"Reverting to your original name? Do forgive me."

"What do you want?"

"I'm here to see the queen."

"I'm here to make sure nothing happens."

Bates smiled. "You expect me to make trouble?"

"Where you go, trouble follows."

"Because I am a part of the human society. If we are to be accepted by them, we must blend in."

"Follow their laws? If you weren't already a doctor, you wouldn't be in the position you're in."

"If I didn't have human helpers, I wouldn't be in the position I'm in."

"Like this soldier?" Petrus focused on Brent. Brent didn't look him in the eye. "Do you realize you are helping a kinslayer?"

Brent said, "He's a friend." As though that statement explained everything.

"I'll bet," said Petrus. He then looked at Bates. "Two minutes."

"I accept," said Bates.

Petrus lead them through the crowd which parted before him. They penetrated the cordon of men who faced out into the crowd. Beyond them, a woman lay across a settee, her hair cut short, her face milk-white and almond-shaped. She had small eyes, small lips, a small pug nose. Her body was alabaster, as if she hadn't eaten.

The woman turned to him, and Brent looked at the wall to avoid her eyes.

The woman stared at Brent. He could feel her eyes trying to catch his own, but he refused to look. He studied the wall behind her.

The woman beckoned and Bates took one step forward. "Sir Arthur Bates," she said. She carefully articulated each syllable. "Who is your soldier?"

"Sergeant Brent Rogers of the Magic Corps."

Petrus snapped, "You bring a wizard in our midst!"

Bates held up his hand. "He's on our side."

"*Your* side, you mean."

"Quiet," said the woman. "You bring a wizard here, which may cause a breach in protocol."

"This is the 21st century, may I remind Your Highness, and times change."

Petrus bristled. Brent stepped closer to Bates. The cordon all turned to face them.

"I have only Your Highness' interests in mind, of course. Your Highness will remember when the Nazis took your convent in France and would have taken you if I had not brought the Druid."

The woman's fangs were out. She did not look happy. "What do you want?"

Bates put a hand on Brent's shoulder. "This human is under my wings. He will not be harmed by any of the kin. In exchange, his magic will be ours."

She ran her tongue across her fangs. Brent found that to be the most erotic motion he had ever seen, and he felt himself stiffen.

Dammit, he swore to himself, and focused on the wall again to force himself to stop the raging hard-on. Then he thought, *He should have asked me, first.* That irritation helped.

"Our own wizard," she said, pondering.

Bates said, "He is still in the Army, so if he is needed it must be for emergencies only. All requests come through me."

Petrus said, "You make a hell of a lot of demands over this little wizard."

Since Petrus wasn't looking at him, Brent focused his attention on him. He had the pale gray eyes of all vampires that fed well. He glared at Bates, who also did not look him in the eye. Bates bowed a little. "Even you must understand how important it is for a queen to have a wizard nearby."

"I could, indeed, be queen in more than name," said the woman.

"Absolutely," said Bates.

She looked to Brent. Petrus did too and Brent dropped his eyes. "Prove he is a wizard."

Brent felt rather than saw the movement on Bates' right, the opposite side of where he stood. He reached out with his hand and his mind, and formed the spell "Raise the Enemy."

A woman shrieked in surprise as she was thrown up in the air and slammed into the ceiling. She threw something at them and it deflected from his shield to skitter across the floor, into the crowd.

"Petrus," said Bates, "Even I could see that com—"

There was another assassin who came full-tilt at Brent. Brent barely turned the shield in time. The man ran into the shield, about two feet away from Brent, just out of arm's length of a metal stake. A stake? Really?

"Enough," said the queen.

The woman fell from the ceiling, falling face-first onto the marble of the ballroom floor. Brent did not even look to see if she was safe.

"I accept your terms for the wizard," said the queen. "However, if he does not survive his tour, all agreements are negated."

"All of them?"

"*All* of them."

Bates looked at Brent. He seemed to be assessing whether Brent would live through two more years. Brent knew he would. The fortune tellers would have told him otherwise.

"The hospital is still a sanctuary?"

"Yes, of course it is."

"Then I agree."

Brent wondered why Bates was so worried.

The queen raised her glass. "Enjoy the party."

Bates bowed his head again. "Thank you." He put a hand on Brent's arm, turned to his right, and they passed through an opening in the cordon.

"Doc—"

"Outside," Bates said sharply, moving toward a set of French doors open to a patio. Brent followed Bates out to the far end of a pool filled with floating candles. He stopped, faced Brent.

"I'm sure you're wondering what the hell I'm doing."

"I've been pimped out to the queen of the vampires."

"One of the many self-styled queens of vampires. She is in charge of the Americas. The middle East right now is in flux, and you're presently stationed in the East—"

"I don't care about the politics."

"You will once I tell you that you now will have a nice fat target on your back."

"Nothing new there, Doc. I'm in tan and look like the rest of the Army. The Taliban can't tell the difference." He was glad it was dark. He could look up at Bates' face and not worry about getting caught in his gaze. "You did pimp me out, didn't you?"

"Looking at it from your point of view, it would seem that way. But remember—they have to go through me. I'm not going to call you for a cat stuck in a tree."

"What's this about a kinslayer?"

He smiled. Brent saw the white teeth. "I killed many vampires. I'm not only a doctor, but I was the queen's assassin."

"This queen?"

"No. Before her. During Petrus' time, when he was still a suckling babe."

"You're older than I thought."

He laughed. "Age means nothing to us. If I were the type to care—which I'm not—I would be in there, jockeying for position in court. To some of the ambitious, that's what's important."

"But because you…killed, you're an outsider."

"Very astute. You learn better than some of those against the wall who have a few decades on you. I may raise you if something untimely happens."

"Please don't." Brent preferred whatever afterlife there was, not an eternity of politicking.

Bates laughed again. "Now we can enjoy the hospitality of the host."

Bates walked back into the party through the large French doors. Brent could do nothing but follow. Again Bates took a glass of the dark drink and sipped it. He paused at the doors, looking out into the crowd.

The room was not as crowded, especially along the walls. Brent saw that the queen, her entourage, and her cordon had left the room. It probably meant she was holding court elsewhere. Bates then started to walk, nodding to people as he walked by, people who did not nod back, but stared at him. He was aiming toward a woman, in a sea-green gown of sequins and pearls. Her long black hair cascaded down her back.

Bates spoke to her in a language that didn't sound European. Brent didn't understand it—it sounded like mostly vowels and soft consonants. She didn't smile, answered him curtly. Bates continued talking to her, gently and kindly. Brent turned his back on the two and kept his eye on the people in the room.

The man who had brought him his dress greens stepped smartly to Brent's side, getting between him and Bates. "How's it goin'," he said.

"Not bad."

The big bald man held out his hand. "Reese." His blue eyes were light, almost translucent like the vampires, but he was fully human, Brent could tell that.

Brent wasn't sure if that was his first or last name. "Brent," he said, shaking the man's hand.

"I know. First time doing the bodyguard thing?"

Brent jockeyed for a position next to Bates. "What gave you that idea?"

Reese did not budge, but he smiled. "Where you're standing, and you're making it obvious where you want to stand."

Bates separated himself from the woman. Reese stepped aside for Bates, so the whole pissing contest was now moot. "Time for us to leave the Children of the Moon to their own devices," Bates said to Brent. He nodded to Reese. "Excuse us."

Reese bowed a little. Bates was already moving toward the side of the room, where a door stood unguarded. Bates casually opened it, and Brent stepped inside with him.

Brent said, "Do you know that guy?"

"He works for me sometimes," said Bates, as he walked down the hall.

They were at the end of a hallway, finely carpeted with portraits on the walls on either side. After the gallery, they took a left and then a side door, which led to the side of the house. The limos were parked there, and the chauffeurs were all gathered around a folding table laden with food. Bates said, "Find Jackson and we'll be on our way."

"And leave you alone out here?"

Bates smiled. "My astute young friend, I haven't survived this long based on luck alone."

"Okay." Brent tried to remember what the chauffeur looked like as they had passed into the battlefield. He decided to approach the picnic table.

"Hey," he said, and the three chauffeurs there looked up at him. "Any of you Jackson?"

"No," said one. "I'll get him." The chauffeur who returned with him was the man Brent remembered from the car.

"Master is leaving?" asked Jackson. He had a high accent at the end of his question—Swedish, perhaps.

"Yeah," said Brent. He didn't think he could ever see himself calling Bates "Master".

"I'll bring the car around the front door."

"Thanks," but Jackson already disappeared into the shadows.

Brent reported to Bates, "He'll be at the front door."

"Very good." They walked the fifty yards or so to the front door of the mansion. The butlers there were surprised to see them come out of the dark. Jackson arrived moments later, and the butler opened the door for Bates to enter. Brent followed.

Bates was putting up the glass partition when Brent got in the limo. It closed, and the air seemed to change, get thicker. Bates turned to him and smiled, fangs showing. "Remember the old days?"

Brent—and his cock—remembered them well. Brent could feel himself start to swell. "This is my dress uniform."

Bates put a hand on Brent's thigh. "Then get out of it." Brent undid the tie and started to unbutton his tunic. Bates helped, and unbuttoned his shirt, parting it.

"Ah," he said appreciatively, "look at you." Although not a body builder, he did go to the gym during downtime. Bates leaned in to Brent's chest and dragged his teeth over Brent's nipple. Brent gasped, his cock probably at full mast now. He knew what was coming next. He could feel Bates unbuttoning his pants, squeezing his swelling member.

Brent let Bates pull down the pants and underwear, and his member popped up to his abdomen. Bates got down from his seat and knelt on the floor, parting Brent's legs. He took a hold of Brent's member and began to stroke it. "You haven't changed," he said. "So hard and ready for me."

Brent, gasping, looked down at Bates. Bates smiled, again, the fangs, and licked his head. Brent moaned, casting his head back onto the seat. Bates expertly wrapped his mouth around Brent and began to suck, taking him all the way down. Brent put a hand in Bates' hair, gripping it. Sometimes he liked to be forced, he had admitted, and Brent was only too happy to oblige. He forced him down, something that would choke a lesser man, but Bates was certainly an expert. Bates didn't need to breathe, so he didn't come up for air, but began to move his head up and down on him. Bates was relentless and constant.

"Fuck," Brent whispered, as he held himself from the brink. "Now."

Bates pulled off and turned to the inside of Brent's thigh. At the same time Brent shot onto his abdomen, Bates bit into the artery of his leg. He felt Bates latch onto him, felt the blood flow, and listened to the deep beating of his own heart and the pleasurable moaning of Bates as he drank.

Bates lifted his head. Brent had many scars on the inside of his leg from this sort of thing. Brent gathered himself together as Bates wiped him off with a handy towel. "Was that worth tonight?"

Brent gave him a cocky grin. "I like that kind of payment."

EIGHT

The oven heated the house to what could normally be unbearable, but after coming from the desert, Brent didn't think it was that bad. It had chased his father out of the house to go man the grill. Brent didn't want another party but his mother made the plans, inviting Lori, the kids, Keithy and his father's partner, since they were on call. Brent headed outside to join his father. The gas grill was smoking with applewood chips; his father, though not a master griller, was like his mother and loved to try new things, using parties as an excuse — though he'd never admit it.

"Is Keithy actually going to come?" Brent asked.

"He said he would." His father shrugged. "You know him and free food."

Brent heard a car pull into the driveway. He turned to see Lori's black Mercedes parking behind the rental. The kids piled out before she even put it in park.

"Grampa!" cried out Kaitlyn, running to him. He turned to guard the grill and caught her. Ashlyn shuffled over, gazing at Brent. She held onto a ratty stuffed tiger, so pale from washings that it was almost all white. Dante roared next onto the scene, pushing Ashlyn violently aside and running into the house. "Food!"

Lori was dressed in a very short sundress with a halter top. She carried a foil-wrapped bowl. "I've got your favorite, Brent. Antipasto."

A salad of peppers, onions, olives, and three different meats and cheeses, Lori's antipasto was expensive, but to die for. She thrust the bowl at Brent. "I got more stuff in the car."

Inside, Dante was perched precariously on the edge of the table. Brent's mother had stopped what she was doing to make a plate for Dante. Brent set the antipasto on the counter. Dante jumped off the table, and took the plate from Brent's mother. He sauntered off to the TV.

There was a blood-curdling girl's scream from outside. Brent and his mother saw Ashlyn, hiding behind her mother, staring at his father who had a helpless look. "She doesn't like being touched, Dad," said Lori patiently.

Ashlyn was whimpering, holding onto the short sundress for dear life.

"You really should get her some help, Lori," said his father sternly. "You can't keep her in that daycare forever."

"Do you know how expensive private schools are?" She glared at Kaitlyn, who looked down. Brent walked back into the house; he wanted to go to his bedroom with Pickles, to wait out the party, and hope no one would miss him.

Another car pulled into the driveway. In the back passenger seat, half hanging out the window, was Keithy, looking white and gasping for air. Brent saw Ty get out of the driver's seat. He stepped outside to call, "Hey, bro." He opened the door for Keithy.

"You didn't tell me the back doors locked," said Keithy, almost panicked.

"Sorry. But the windows rolled down."

"Half way."

"Next time sit in the front seat."

"Are there airbags?"

"Yeah."

Brent rolled his eyes as Keithy kept asking safety questions. Ty didn't know what the rating was for a side crash. No, there weren't any side airbags. "They don't make that."

"They should. Where's the food?"

"In the house," said Brent.

Keithy stumbled past Brent, avoiding the picnic table in the back. Brent shook his head. "Piece of fucking work."

Ty shrugged. "I did my job. He might make you give him a ride, since your car's newer."

"Great," said Brent.

Ty held out his hand. "I'll see you later."

"You're not staying?"

"No, I just gave him a ride."

"You can stay if you want."

"You sure?"

"It's sort of my party. I can invite who I want."

Ty chuckled. "All right. Thanks."

"C'mon, I'll introduce you."

Brent did so, leaving Lori for last. She batted her eyelashes at Ty and acted sweet. Her halter top barely hid her breasts. Brent was surprised at his sister's reaction to Ty.

Hamburgers and hot dogs came out, along with ribs — wet and dry — corn, a few appetizer concoctions with mayonnaise and cheese as bases. As soon as everyone sat down, another car came in. This was a Lincoln Crown Vic, screaming "cop car." Brent couldn't see the man get out, but did see him come to the table.

Tall, thin, and lanky, he looked like a plastic man that had been pulled too far. His legs were long and thin, his hands were almost to his knees. He had brown hair with gray accents, and mud-brown eyes. He had a tired, haggard look, even when he smiled.

"Hey, Luke, glad you could make it. Everyone, this is my partner, Lucas Petreault."

Everyone said hi. Lori wasn't attracted to him, because she didn't bat her eyelashes at him. Her eyes wide in wonder, Ashlyn hung onto mother. Kaitlyn stared at him. Dante didn't care. Brent shook the man's hand—it was warm and clammy. When Luke spoke, his voice was an octave higher than any man's speaking voice. "I am glad to be here."

"Help yourself," said his mother.

He picked up a plate, and took modest amounts. He sat down next to Kaitlyn who squeezed close to her grandmother.

Lori, who hated dead air, asked Ty what he did. Putting down his hamburger, he wiped his mouth before answering. "Right now, I work for UPS as a packer/shipper."

"You might have handled packages from me," she said with a smile.

"Maybe," he replied.

"Ever have to go to Lynnfield?"

"No, I'm in the Worcester plant."

"Oh. That's where the ex's family is." She took a hot dog without a bun. "Ex, you know. I'm divorced. Four years."

"I see."

"How's the burger?" interrupted Brent's father.

"Excellent," said Ty with a smile. "Is it smoked?"

Brent's father beamed. "Yes!" He talked about what wood he used, and assorted grilling information, more than anyone needed to know. Luke was quiet, observing all that went on around him. It wasn't until he spoke that people noticed he was there. He seemed to have disappeared while sitting right in front of them.

Brent's mom got a bottled water for him. Brent asked him, "How long have you been on the force?"

"I am on an exchange," said Luke. "I'm from Marseille, in France."

"You don't have an accent," said Ty, saying what Brent was thinking.

"My past is, ah, complicated."

Then Dante demanded more food, and Luke seemed to retreat. What itched Brent's mind was how he became part of the woodwork.

After lunch came the Peanut Butter Fudge pie, which his mom had slaved over. Thick and creamy, Brent took a large slice of his favorite dessert.

As they dug into it, Brent heard a beeper go off. His father and Luke pulled out their beepers. "It's the office," Luke said.

"I'll change," said Brent's father.

Luke took out his cell and started dialing in. He excused himself to go near the dog run, out of earshot of the people there. Pickles followed, thinking he had food.

The party broke up soon after Brent's father and Luke left. In about 20 minutes, everyone was gone, leaving Brent, his mom, and Pickles. Brent helped his mom clean up, gave her a running commentary of the food, which was excellent as always. Then he went to his room with Pickles and fell asleep.

NINE

Brent's father didn't get home until long after Brent headed to bed for the night, and left before sunrise the next morning. He waited until ten before calling Chrissie. She answered on the third ring. "I knew it was you, Magic Man."

He liked her nickname for him. "Are you a telepath now?"

"No, just good at guessing. I'm available tonight."

"What would you like to go see?"

"How do you like Brad Pitt?"

"I can take him or leave him."

"Well, you're lucky that *The Notebook* didn't open last weekend or I'd drag you to that."

"Please. Something that won't put me to sleep."

"Then it's Brad Pitt in *Troy*."

"Sounds good. What time?"

She said, "6:12. Dinner at four again? Or lunch and the afternoon show?"

"Lunch sounds better. Pick you up in an hour."

He knew she'd want to have an early lunch. He brought her to Jake's. It wasn't busy on a Monday. They had meatloaf, which Brent would admit, was better than his mother could ever make.

Chrissie told stories of Wal-Mart that cracked him up, and he told war stories. War between patrols was boring, and when there's a bunch of guys with nothing to do, there were bound to be pranks of all sorts. After that, they drove to the mall for the nearest movie and made the 1:30 showing.

The war scenes made Brent grip the chairs. He had seen something like Greek Fire in action, seen the RPG's and explosions, seen the army camps and men gathered, bored. He saw them looking, always looking for Taliban.

They're not looking for Taliban here. But if they had wizards, they would have wiped the Greeks off the map. It took him until the very end to calm down. Chrissie noticed, but sat in the seat, not rushing him through the credits. He finally looked at her, reached over and took her hand.

"You okay?" she asked.

"Yeah."

"I'm not the only one with issues, it seems."

"It's not that bad."

She only smiled at him. "Okay."

He got up, still holding her hand. They left, hand in hand. She didn't seem to mind. He escorted her to the passenger side of the car, and they stood, staring at each other.

Finally, she stood on her toes and kissed him. A peck at first, and then a long, deep, soulful kiss. He responded, pulling her close to him. He broke off, looked at her cornflower blue eyes. "That was very nice," he said, smiling.

"It's been so long, I thought I forgot how."

"It's like riding a bike. You don't forget."

She stepped out of his embrace, looking shyly away, and got into his car. He was still smiling as he got into the driver's seat and drove her home. They shared another kiss outside of Keithy's apartment house. "Know any spells that can make me have sex with you?" she asked him.

"Technically no. We're not allowed to force emotions on people."

She touched his nose with a fingertip. "I'm going to hold you to that."

"Spells are more effective on the willing. All my spell would do is give a nudge."

"Do you think I need a nudge?"

"I think you don't want to get hurt," he said.

"My goodness, Magic Man, you read my mind."

"I'm situationally astute," he said.

She laughed, patted his arm. "Thursday?"

"I'll be there."

She got out of the car, and instead of going around the corner like the first night, She walked into Keithy's apartment house. He was curious. Was she going to tell Keithy what a great—or shitty—time she had? She wouldn't have asked to get together Thursday if it was shitty, though.

He drove away, wondering why she had gone to Keithy's place. Unless, of course, she lived there, which would explain Lori's statement that Keithy was going after the girl upstairs, and how she came over that first day they met, carrying groceries for Keithy.

Brent smiled. "Situationally astute, indeed."

✫　　✫　　✫

He didn't want to go home at the moment. He pulled into the Red Bar. He wasn't sure why, but he sat in the car for a few minutes, thinking of how happy Chrissie made him; much happier than Sarah, that was for certain.

He looked in the rear-view mirror and watched as a Yugo drove into the parking lot. The car parked far away from the door, backing carefully into a spot. Brent watched the man get out, unfolding himself from the small car.

It was Luke. Brent thought back to yesterdays' barbecue. Brent noticed Luke had said hardly anything, content with watching everyone else. If he hadn't sat across from Brent, he'd have forgotten that he was even there. This meant, to Brent, that there was something not quite human about him.

Brent got out of the car. Luke stopped walking, moved his entire body to face Brent. "You are Brent, yes?"

"Yes," Brent said, leaning on his trunk. "How are you, Luke?"

"Good." He tilted his head. "Is there something I can do for you?"

"I'd like to shake your hand."

Luke smiled. It was wan and tired. "I know what you can do. You have met many Children of the Moon, I am sure?"

"Well, yes."

"I assure you, I am not one of those." He walked over to Brent. "I also assure you, that although I may not look human, I am truly a human being. A freak yes, but a human nonetheless."

"But—you disappear."

"I blend in. When one is as freakish as I, one should blend in, no?"

Brent rubbed the back of his neck. Something about the man didn't seem right to him. He wasn't sure if Luke was lying,

130

misleading, or genuinely believing he was something that he wasn't. Brent wasn't about to apologize, though. He was sure he was right.

Luke spread his hands. "What more do you want?"

"Tell me about your past. You said it was complicated."

Again, he sighed. "I was given to the church when I was a baby," he said. "I was brought up in the boys' choir. I sang, beautifully, giving grace to God." He leaned closer to Brent. "They wanted me to keep the sweet lark's voice."

Brent looked up at the man's eyes. They were light blue, not translucent like a vampire's. However, Brent wasn't sure what Luke was getting at. "I don't understand."

"To make a lark continue with its tender voice, you castrate him."

Brent got butterflies in his groin. "You mean—"

Luke only nodded.

Which explained his high voice, his dainty hands, his feminine face. Brent forced himself not to look down. "I'm—oh."

Luke shrugged "I have made my peace with God and man." He stepped back. "You understand now?"

The apology came out quickly. "I'm sorry I misjudged you."

"It is a common misunderstanding. Many people mistake me for a Child of the Moon. I have been called *Fee*—fairy."

"I can see that."

"Now, will you come in for a drink?"

"No, I think I've bothered you enough." He paused. "Does my father know?"

"Of course."

His father was always a good keeper of secrets, Brent realized.

"You must understand this is not something I broadcast."

"I understand." But it was creepy. Very creepy.

⭐   ⭐   ⭐

He saw the car on the side of the road and did a double-take. He passed it, just to be sure, and then turned around in a parking lot. He turned around again and parked right behind the car.

Sarah ran to the side window. "Oh," she said, her face falling. "Hello."

"Stuck?"

"Yeah."

He got out of the car. "Battery dead?"

"I don't know. I was driving along and I heard a *thunk*."

She had the hood open. He didn't know much about cars. Unfortunately, his ability didn't extend to machines, except to sense them to blow them up. They didn't teach him much vehicle magic in the Corps, either. "Your engine light come on?"

"No." She looked uncomfortable. "I called Boz. He'll be here soon."

He didn't wince. That was good. "Don't know what to tell you," he said. Then, a big black truck pulled up ahead of them. There were ladders and plywood in the back of the truck.

Three people got out. One was Boz. "What the fuck you doin' here?" he snarled at Brent.

"I saw her on the side of the road and thought she needed help," he said.

"We don't need any of your help."

One of the construction guys was heading directly behind Brent. Brent backed up into him. The guy grabbed his shoulder and shoved him hard toward the sidewalk. Brent tripped over the curb and stumbled onto the sidewalk. "Jesus Christ, you guys on 'roids or something?"

"Fuck you," said the construction guy and took a swing. It missed by a mile, and Brent mentally shoved him against the truck.

Then he got a blinding pain in the back of his head that radiated immediately to his eyes, seeing stars. He crumpled to the ground.

He couldn't focus, his head hurt too much. Someone was yelling but he didn't understand the words. He tried to get to his hands and knees but his muscles wouldn't work.

Someone hit him on the side and he fell sideways to the ground, his head bouncing on concrete. He thought about raising his head, and that was his last thought.

TEN

"How long have I been out?" Brent asked the nurse who checked his vitals.

"You've been here since seven, so about eight hours. Any pain?"

"My head hurts like the devil." He lay back on the pillow.

"You have a concussion and a fractured rib," she said. "Try not to move around too much."

"I was safer in Afghanistan," he said.

The nurse laughed. "You don't expect to need body armor around here." She looked at his eyes. "You might be here until shift-change for observation." She entered the data she had collected into the computer near the door.

He closed his eyes. It didn't help.

"There's a policeman outside. Are you up for visitors?"

"Sure," he said, opening his eyes.

"I'll see if the doctor can give something for the pain. We might do an MRI or CAT scan to see if there's any swelling."

"Okay, thanks." She left, and the two patrolmen entered. Brent smiled, knowing them both. "Hey, Butch, Lenny."

"Hey kiddo," said Butch, a young, chiseled man with dark hair and eyes. He had biceps as big as Brent's calves.

Lenny had lighter hair, lighter eyes, and lighter coloring. He had a notebook out.

Butch said, "So, got clocked, didn't you?"

"Yeah."

"Do you know who did it?"

"No. They were three guys from a construction crew."

Lenny scribbled.

Butch continued, "The girl at the scene said she thought you were some homeless guy, passed out on the sidewalk. She didn't know who you were. She didn't see any guys, either."

Bitch! His mind screamed. He couldn't believe it. The very last torch he carried for Sarah died.

"She did, did she? I guess she didn't see me try to help her, either. Or my rental parked behind her."

"It's what she said, it's not what we believed," said Lenny.

Butch said, "We couldn't arrest her on lying."

"Here's what really happened." Brent told them the story from his point of view, while Butch asked questions. Boz aided and abetted. So did Sarah. The two other guys who did the punching would be charged with assault—that is, if Brent wanted to press charges. He said, "No. I don't."

"What?"

Brent sighed. "I want to put this all behind me. Have nothing to do with my ex-girlfriend, her fiancé, or anyone else."

The nurse returned, his mother in tow. His mother nodded to the police; they nodded back. "If you change your mind, call us," said Butch, and left, while his mother rushed to him. "What happened?"

"I got jumped," said Brent. That was the story he stuck with.

After the MRI (which was the most claustrophobic experience of his life) came out normal his mother asked for a doctor's note in case he didn't feel up to returning to duty after his three weeks were over. Brent knew what his mother was trying to do. He was ready to go back.

He got home after sunrise on Tuesday morning. His father was already out to work, and his mother still headed to work after leaving him alone in the house. He was glad they had gone, especially if they were going to see what he was going to do—they'd call him crazy.

Brent winced as Pickles bumped up against his ribs. He let the dog out and walked out to the back yard. Pickles was put out in his dog run, while Brent tried to lay down on the grass. His ribs hurt like hell, and his head had dulled to an ache. Brent dug his fingers into the dirt, feeling the life and energy of the grass and earth. One of the teachers in the magic school was a Wiccan, who taught all the students basic self-healing Earth magic. Though most of the students liked staring at her, Brent took what she said seriously. This wasn't the first time he'd used Earth magic to heal himself.

He took three deep breaths and was instantly in trance. He felt the red aura around the back of his head. An injury there, severe. He let the cooling Earth energy slowly take away the pain and the injury until he felt it become as normal as the rest of him. He then felt the red around his ribs, and slowly lifted a hand, pressing his hand to the area. He gathered his will from the Earth, sending energy to fill the red spot. He had done this to enough soldiers to know how to fix a broken or fractured bone. It was easy and quick to fix.

He finished, taking three more deep breaths which didn't hurt this time. He kept his eyes closed as he let his energy settle, seep back into the Earth. Touching the magic made him again miss using it. He let go of the dirt with his other hand and opened his eyes to a cloudless blue sky. Pickles sat in his dog run, waiting patiently for him.

He got the dog and took a shower, made lunch, hung around with Pickles. His mother stumbled in the door, exhausted. His father followed behind.

"Brent," his father said, "Someone's outside for you."

Brent walked to the porch and looked out the slatted window. Reese stood outside, casually waiting. Brent waved, the man waved back, and he got his formal greens from the closet. "Hey," he said to Reese, bringing the clothes outside.

"Hey," the man replied with a curt nod.

"Did you actually get these for me?"

"Yes. Afghanistan's nice country. A pothead's dream."

Brent laughed. "You noticed."

Reese had no expression as he took the clothes. Brent's laugh faded. "Thanks for doing this for me."

"Sure." Reese started to walk away.

Brent called, "Hey, how's my team?"

"Still there."

"Tell them I should be back soon."

"Sure," Reese said, and got into his car.

Back in the house, his mother sat listlessly at the kitchen table, the plates and utensils in front of her. "Why don't you go to bed, Ma?" Brent asked.

She looked up at Brent. "You look better."

"Thanks." He patted Pickles who ate his food near the kitchen table. "You should go rest."

She shook her head. "I'll eat first."

He passed the platter of leftover pork ribs for everyone and watched as his mother took two bites and closed her eyes. She fell asleep right there.

His father shook his head. "Stubborn. Maggie. Honey? Go to bed."

She came out of it and said, "Yeah, maybe I'd better. I'm sorry, honey."

"Don't be," said Brent, as his mother got up. She stumbled to the bedroom.

His father turned to him. "You're not pressing charges?"

"I hit him first, Dad."

"You don't deserve the beating you got."

Brent raised his hands. "I don't want to escalate this. I just want it to go away."

Someone beeped a horn outside. Brent frowned. "Now what?" He got up, leaving his dinner on the table. He looked out the windows and saw the blue car in his driveway. He stepped outside, barefoot on the asphalt. "George," he said, when he got out of the car.

"Hey," he said. Pickles bounded up to him. George scratched him behind the ears. "I—um, how are you?"

"Better."

"Why? What happened?"

"Boz's construction crew jumped me yesterday."

"No shit?"

"No shit."

"What're you going to do?"

"Nothing."

"Dude. They jumped you."

"I started it. I'm a bigger man than that." He crossed his arms. "What's up?"

George looked uncomfortable. "I want—um, you're right."

"About?"

"Me turning into my step-father. I've been drinking too much."

"Are you going to stop?"

"I can't. I'll cut down. I didn't have a drink until noon."

Brent didn't want to know how much he used to drink before noon. "That's good, right?"

George nodded. "I was drinking more than my stepdad."

"At least you're stopping before you wrap your car around a tree."

"Yeah." He laughed. "Am I interrupting anything?"

"Only dinner. Want to come in?"

"Sure it's okay?"

He nodded. "I made enough for four. It's habit."

George followed Brent into the house. His father had paused eating. "Hey, George."

"Mr. Rogers."

"Mind if he joins us?" asked Brent.

"I got a call in. You can sit here." His father took his plate away and dropped it in the sink. "Tell Mom I'm out."

"Okay," said Brent, as his father grabbed his suit jacket and left.

Brent served George, and gave him lemonade to drink, which he drank like a man dying of thirst. They shared small talk, not about the attack or about George's alcoholism. After dinner, George helped dry the dishes, and they sat outside in the relatively cooler air under the mosquito-netted gazebo. George was looking at something beyond the driveway. "You know that guy?" he asked, pointing to a white Escalade parked half in front of his driveway.

"No idea."

"He's been there since I came here."

Brent, if he wanted, could blow out the windows, pick up the Escalade and shake whoever it was out, or he could tear open the doors. If it was a bad guy, he could do these things. But this wasn't in-country, and he couldn't do that here, in the US, no matter how threatened he felt. "Be right back," he said, and started walking barefoot toward the Escalade.

It very slowly started down the street, reluctant to leave but knowing it had to. Brent stood in the middle of his driveway, now confused.

"Did you see who it was?"

Brent shook his head. "No, but they didn't want to talk to me."

"Drug dealers?"

"Wouldn't be surprised."

ELEVEN

The next morning, he was awakened at eight by his phone ringing. He answered it, trying to keep the sleepiness out of his voice. "Hello?"

"Hey, Magic Man, did I wake you up?"

"No, not really."

"Oh, okay. Well, I'm working tomorrow. Are you doing anything today?"

"I have no plans."

"Want to go to Boston?"

"Sure. I haven't been there in a while."

"I'll drive. My car's not as fancy as yours. But it'll get us there and back."

That reminded him. "I have to find out where my car went to."

She laughed. "You don't know where your car is?"

"I stopped to help someone and I think they towed it."

"Better get on that. I'll pick you up in an hour?"

"Sure, that sounds good." He launched himself out of bed and headed to the shower while dialing the rental agency. The police had towed the car back to the rental agency, and he could come down today to get a new one.

He sat on the stairs at the front door to wait for Chrissie to show up. Her car was an older model Camry, silver but without any body rot that he could see. He climbed into the passenger side. He put his seat belt on and looked around the inside. "It's a nice car."

She shrugged. "Gets me places. Did you find your car?"

"It's at the rental agency. I need to pick up a new one, if you don't mind driving me there."

"Sure. Is it at the airport?"

"Yeah."

"Damn. Okay."

"Is there anything wrong?"

"I don't like the tunnel. All that water above us…"

"Don't worry. I'll get us through."

She smiled.

He asked, "Do you need to go to Boston for a reason?"

"No reason. I like the shops. If I have some extra money, I go there."

"Most people go to the mall."

She laughed. "Have you no knowledge of girls? We go where the fancy stuff is, not just the mall."

"Obviously my manual needs updating."

"Your brother's been acting weird toward me," she said after a short time of listening to the rock station on the radio. "If I didn't know better, I'd think he was jealous."

"He is," Brent said. "He always was."

"Oh, you always got the girl?" She grinned at him.

"I got the girl that he thought he wanted. They ended up not being what I wanted. A couple of them went out with him, but, well, they weren't as smart as you."

"You liked airheads?"

"I was young, stupid, on the rebound. I was trying to make my ex jealous but it was like she didn't even see me."

"And now?"

"Now?" He suddenly felt the empty pit where his heart was, but it seemed to be a lot less of a weight with Chrissie around. "I don't want anything to do with her. She never sent me letters, never talked to me when I called. It's like I was a non-person."

"Girls do that. Burn bridges."

"What about you?"

"Me? Didn't I tell you I was a lesbian?"

"Not by the way you kissed me."

"All a ruse. Okay, not really. It's been a while."

"You do have the rule of not putting out on the first date."

"I mean to stand by it, too. Look, there's a double standard. Guys do it on a first date and they're conquerors. Girls do it and they're sluts. Am I right?"

"I can see that point," Brent said. "But with guys, it's all about the sex."

"You don't seem to be that way."

He smiled. "Seem."

"Ah. You're getting it on the side."

He laughed and hoped she didn't see him blush.

"The Army is celibate?"

"Have I gotten it while I was in the Army? Or recently since I've been home, you mean?"

"I can't believe you're telling me about your sex life."

"Why not? I think I should be up front and honest, don't you?"

"Well, it is — refreshing." She glanced at him. He smiled at her. She had both hands on the wheel or he would have taken one, held it, kissed it.

"Anything other than sex you're interested in?" he asked.

"Magic School is classified—Oh, I love this song!" She cranked up a Van Halen song. They both sang along with it, laughing afterward. A little while after the song, she sighed, "Mom says I'm selfish because I didn't move down to Florida with them. Pete, my brother, he's going to kill her someday and it'll be my fault."

"Because you're not there to take the bullet?"

"Knife. We have to keep them away from him."

"Jesus. Don't they have institutions for people like him?"

"Nobody will take him. He's too violent."

Brent thought they should put people like that away, but he didn't dare express it.

They got off in Cambridge. She parked the car on a side street about three blocks from Union Square.

"I thought you didn't like school."

"I don't. But the stores here are cool." They walked along Somerville Avenue, hand in hand, looking at the different shops. They got an expensive coffee and kept walking. It started getting crowded at lunch, so they looked for a restaurant that wasn't busy. They found a Mexican restaurant. The food there was not bad, too much cheese, but they didn't care. Brent was happy that Chrissie didn't care. "I'll pay for it at the gym later," she said.

They walked back to the car, with nothing in hand. "We'll try Faneuil Hall," she said.

"Okay," he said, and got in. She turned the key and nothing happened.

"Shit," Chrissie spat.

"What?" Brent asked.

She turned the key again. "Know any magic for cars?" She kept trying, pumping the gas to the floor.

"Don't do that, you'll flood it."

"Flood what?"

"I don't know. My father used to tell me that."

She stopped. "Shit." She turned to him. "Do you have triple-A?"

"Not anymore."

"Shit." She turned back at the steering wheel.

"So," he said. "Call a tow? Do they take cards?"

"I don't know. I doubt it." She took out her cell and called someone. "Jenny? Yeah. I need a tow. No, I'm in Somerville. Can you get me the number of a tow truck?" She headed back into the car and tore open the glove box. Rifling through it she found a pen and grabbed a piece of paper from the floor. "Okay, go. Yep…yep…okay. Thanks." She called the number and asked if they took cards, and then told them where she was. "They'll be here in fifteen minutes or so," she said, hanging up and looking to Brent. "I'm sorry."

"It's not your fault," he said. "I can pay for it."

"No, I have my emergency credit card here."

"Maybe he can give us a ride to the airport. I'll pick up the car and we can go to Faniuel Hall."

She cleaned up the stuff she had pulled out of her glove box until the tow truck driver got there. He double-parked next to the car. "Hey," he called from the open window. He was a little older than Brent, heavy set with a beard. "What's up?" He talked to Brent, ignoring Chrissie.

Chrissie visibly bristled. "Excuse me," she said, "It's my car."

"Oh." The mechanic parked and got out.

"It won't start."

He looked back at Brent, who shrugged. The mechanic said, "Go start it," as he walked around to the front of the engine. She unlocked the hood for him as he lifted it.

She tried to start it. Both men heard a clicking sound in the engine. "I think you need a jump. Hold on." The mechanic gut a set of jumper cables and attached them. "Try again."

Said Brent, "It sounds like it wants to."

"Not enough juice," said the mechanic. "Might be the battery or the alternator, too."

Brent winced, knowing that an alternator was a lot of money. The mechanic told her to stop. "Your engine light ever go on?"

"No," she said, getting out. "What's the verdict?"

"I'll have to look at it, but I think it's your electrical system."

She sighed. "Great."

The mechanic slammed shut the hood, and looked around. "I have to get it out of this parking spot." There were cars tightly parked both in front and behind her.

"I can do that," said Brent.

The mechanic said, "How're you gonna do that?"

Brent smiled. "Just move your truck up." Brent turned to Chrissie and put his arm around Chrissie's waist. "Are you ready to see some magic?"

She didn't look like she was in the mood for tricks.

Brent closed his eyes and called the magic, the power and his own ability. He slowly raised his hands, and the car lifted as he opened his eyes. The car floated up in the air, about a foot off the ground. Brent waved a hand, and the car moved sideways, out of the parking spot and into the street. He carefully positioned it right behind the tow truck.

The mechanic stood still as the car settled on the ground. He looked at the car, then Brent, who didn't even break a sweat. "Shit," the man said.

"Can you give us a ride?"

"Where?"

"We need to get to the airport."

The man looked again at the car. Then again at Brent. He seemed to be apprehensive. "I can't. Rules."

Brent was flowing with magic and could easily have forced the guy to take them. "How are we going to get to the airport?"

"Can you fly?"

Chrissie burst out laughing. Brent narrowed his eyes at the mechanic as the magic dissipated. "No, I can't fly."

"I dunno. Take the bus from Union Square?"

"Great," he said. "Thanks."

He started hooking up the car. "Fifty dollars for the tow."

"I got it," both Chrissie and Brent said, but Chrissie was faster, handing over the card.

"I have to call this in," he said.

"Okay."

The man used his radio and called in the card number while Chrissie waited. She put her hand on Brent's arm. "You okay?"

"Can I fly? Jesus."

She snickered. The mechanic called over, "Want me to mail the receipt or do you want to pick it up with the car?"

"I'll pick it up with the car," said Chrissie. "Do you have a business card?"

"Sure," the man fished in his pocket for a business card and handed it to her. Then he finished hooking up the car. "Give me a call in a couple of hours."

"Will do," she said. "Thanks."

"No problem, miss."

As he drove away, Brent looked down the street. "Union Square to Logan airport?"

"I'm sure we'll need a transfer."

"A what?"

"Transfer, to go from one bus to another." She put her arm through his. "Never rode a bus before?"

"School bus," he said.

She laughed. "Follow me."

When they got to Union Square, they grabbed the first bus that arrived, but the bus driver didn't know what bus to take to Logan. Chrissie pulled Brent off before he did something rash.

A woman who was waiting for another bus said, "Get to South Station, and you can take a shuttle to the airport."

So the next bus was going to Massachusetts Institute of Technology, also known as MIT. "You can get to South Station from here," said the new bus driver, much more friendly than the first. They got off at MIT. There were a series of schedules posted on the walls. Through the graffiti on the plastic protecting the schedules from the weather, they saw they needed bus 78 to get to South Station. They couldn't see the times, though.

"I guess we wait," said Brent, sitting down on the bench.

"I wouldn't sit there," said Chrissie.

Brent jumped up, looked at the bench. She laughed. "You never know what was there."

"I guess you're right." He remained standing up. The kiosk got full of people and when bus 78 came, they all seemed to queue up for it. Brent found himself standing all the way to South Station. He was sorely tempted to put up force fields to keep people away from him and Chrissie, but as the bus kept picking up passengers, the more crowded it got. Finally, after what seemed like hours, they pulled into South Station. Brent got out and gasped for air. "This is why I drive," he said, checking his pockets.

"I thought that you'd get used to that smell in the Army."

"Get used to what? We all smell that bad."

She smiled and took his hand. "Shuttles are over here." She seemed to be more familiar with South Station, so he basically followed her. She got a schedule, found what they needed, and guided him to the shuttle. He felt helpless as he surrendered himself. "I'm glad I have you," he said, while they waited. "I'd never find my way around."

"Bet you weren't thinking that when the car didn't start," she said with a grin.

"Hopefully it won't be major."

"It will be. This is Boston. I'm a girl. Even if it's not major, it's going to be expensive."

"If you need help—"

"Don't," she said, and planted a kiss on his lips. "Don't even offer."

The shuttle arrived and they got on. This time, there weren't any smelly people, it was air conditioned and cool, wasn't packed, so they could sit down. When they got to the car rental area, after picking up people at the assorted terminals, they disembarked. Now he was someplace he could control.

At the counter, he was able to talk them into an upgrade to an SUV. Comfortable, in control again, he got behind the wheel. He sighed gratefully as Chrissie got in. "Feel better now that you're not among the great unwashed?"

"Was I that obvious?"

"You were."

He didn't feel as happy anymore. "I'm sorry."

"Don't apologize to me. It didn't bother me." She took out the card. "I'll call them when I get home."

"Hopefully they won't screw you."

"They will. I'm a girl."

✯　　✯　　✯

They got on Route 90 and started back to Worcester. The trip was silent most of the way, listening to satellite radio from the car and trying to find a good station out of the hundred or so available. They sang along with songs, laughed as an old song came on. They were both in a much better mood by the time they got home.

Chrissie said, "All things considered, I had a great time."

"I did too."

"Want to come up to the apartment?"

He threw the SUV into park. "I'd love to."

They got out, and headed to Keithy's apartment house. "I live on the third floor," she said, sheepish. "I didn't want you to know in case you were one of those stalker psychos."

"I understand."

They walked up hand in hand to her apartment. The stairwell was clean of debris and people, and it didn't look any different than it did last week. She opened her door. Brent said, "You know Keithy has a party here every week?"

"Trust me, I know." She threw open the door. "Tada!"

It was sparsely furnished. They were smack-dab in the living room. She immediately kicked off her shoes and pointed to the couch. Brent reached over and took her in his arms. She smiled. They kissed, long and passionate, while she tucked her hands under his shirt at his back. He broke the kiss, taking off his shirt.

"All you magic-types look like this?" she asked, her hand tracing down his chest.

"Some," he said, and tugged at her shirt. She took the hem and pulled it off, and he unhooked her bra. He slowly brought the straps forward as she impatiently shrugged out of it. She grabbed his head and kissed him again, hungry, wanting. He gave it right back to her, knowing now what she wanted.

He kissed along her neck, stopping at her breasts, small but perked up, nipples sticking forward. He took one in his mouth and she moaned, rubbing his hair. He lifted his head and she took his hand, bringing him to the couch.

She stood, half naked in the dim windowless room. She smiled. "Got a raincoat, Magic Man?"

He smiled, pulled out his wallet. "Army issue," he said, taking out a green foil package. It was probably a year old. *Still good*, he thought. He hoped.

She laughed and undid her jeans. He watched as she slipped them off her hips, and bent down to push them off. He pushed down his tented shorts, his member standing straight out when released. She walked over to him. "It's been a while," she said.

"It's like riding a bike." He kissed her, pulled her body to his. Her hands roamed everywhere—his back, his butt, and his cock. He groaned in the kiss as she hefted it. She thumbed his head and he thrust into her hand. She pulled away, went to the couch and lay down, one leg up, the other foot on the floor, spreading herself wide. He got out the condom and slipped it on in record speed, then climbed on top of her.

"Do it," she whispered.

He moved his hips, rubbing himself against her. She was slick, ready for him. Then he moved his hips again and easily slipped inside her. Both moaned at the connection, then laughed at the same time.

He paused, settling inside her, but she wrapped her legs around him. Another hot kiss as he thrust slowly into her. He broke from the kiss, concentrating on his thrusting—then his pounding as she cried out once, and it slipped into a murmur as he kept going, thankful for the condom keeping him up. He felt his balls crawl up, tighten, his body tensed. He groaned, pulsing and shooting into the latex. He closed his eyes, leaning forward but still holding himself up. He felt Chrissie caress his cheek.

"That was nice," she said.

"Not great, earth-moving, awesome?" He opened his eyes, smiling down at her.

"Try it again and let's see."

"I only had the one."

"Drug store's down the street."

"That means I have to go."

"Decisions, decisions."

He chuckled. "Not yet." He kissed her again.

TWELVE

Brent, only in his shorts, got the morning paper for her. He looked up at the balcony and saw Keithy sitting outside.

"Morning!" Brent waved up at him.

Keithy turned around and stormed back into his apartment.

Brent chuckled, walked back inside. He thought about rubbing it in even more as he paused on the second floor. He decided, though, that it was too early in the morning for such a confrontation and headed upstairs.

Keithy's door opened, though. "So," he called after Brent, "still on the love 'em and leave 'em circuit?"

Brent froze. "I don't know what you're talking about," he called down the stairs.

"Sure, you do. You'll fuck her and dream of goody two-shoes Sarah. If that bitch called you, you'd go crawling like a dog back to her."

Brent backed down the stairs. "You got that all wrong."

"Oh, let me guess. You love Chrissie?"

"I like her a lot. We might go out, who knows."

Keithy stood in the doorway, so angry his jowls shook. "She's going to come crying on my shoulder when you fuck her over."

"Then congratulations, you win." He headed upstairs while Keithy slammed shut his apartment door.

He opened the door, making a point to shut it quietly instead of slamming it. He passed through the living room into the kitchen where a stack of pancakes waited for him.

"You spoil me," he said, looping an arm around her waist.

She wore a large t-shirt that had a cartoon character in a strait-jacket and underneath it read, "You say asylum like it's a bad thing." "Eat while it's hot, then get out of my house," she said, kissing him.

"Going to join me?"

"I have a few more to make." She flipped over the ones in the pan.

"I'm in the Army, not the whole Army," he said. He took half the stack.

"You're a growing boy." She saw what was left and shut off the stove. "I guess the birds will eat them."

He motioned to the only other mismatched kitchen chair. "Sit."

"Sir, yes, sir." She saluted and sat down.

"If you're going to do that, I'm going to have to teach you to do it right."

"I did it wrong?"

"It was sloppy. Scrub the toilet with a toothbrush."

"They really do that?"

"I was on my hands and knees for two hours, scrubbing the grout in the showers. Believe me, that was light."

"They do crazy things in boot camp, I hear."

"The Marines are worse, they say, which gives them their attitude."

"When do you want to do this again?"

He smiled. "Tomorrow? After the party?"

"We can scream and no one will notice."

He laughed. "All right. I'll probably be here for the party, anyway." He could blend into the crowd and have a few beers at Keithy's expense while waiting.

Brent ate his pancakes with bad coffee. It seemed she was a tea drinker and couldn't make a cup of coffee to save her life. He ended up leaving her apartment at nine. He couldn't stop smiling as he drove home.

THIRTEEN

The next night, he was back at the apartment house with the party in full swing again. He told his mother he wouldn't be home tonight again. His mother didn't look happy at that. "Please be careful," she told him.

He squeezed his way up the stairs to Keithy's apartment. Ty was in the doorway, as if waiting for him. He grinned as Brent stepped out of the crowd. "Hey there," he said, slapping Brent on the back. "I didn't know if you were going to make it."

"Yeah, I'm a little late. Less chance of getting too drunk."

"I'll get you a beer," said Ty, ducking into the apartment. He soon came out with two cold bottles, sweat dripping from them enticingly. Brent took the offered bottle and drank deeply. The Bud tasted a bit like a stout to him, but it was cold and wet while the stairwell was hot and crowded.

Ty led him to the third floor stairwell where they had sat before. They sat and drank the beer. "Tough week?" asked Ty.

"It's been one of those weeks, yeah." He glanced at Chrissie's door. "Does the person who lives up here even bother you guys?"

"Nope." He drank while Brent finished his. That went down smooth. Too smooth. Brent gazed at the empty bottle.

It swam in and out of focus. Was he drunk already? He looked up at Ty, who was watching him intently. "You don't look so good. Want me to take you home?"

Brent opened his mouth to speak but couldn't seem to form words. He tried to look down, but moved so slowly that he wondered if he moved at all.

Hangover. Hangover spell. What's the spell?

He couldn't think of the spell, never mind say the words or perform the action.

"I better take you home, man," said Ty, putting Brent's arm around his shoulder and hauling him up. Brent could not move his feet, so Ty had to carry him down the stairs and out the door. Ty brought him to his own car, and poured Brent into the passenger seat.

Ty got in the driver's side. "You should be more careful, man," he said, starting up the car. As he drove, Brent tried to move again, but this time he couldn't move at all. He couldn't move his head. He tried to speak but could only exhale.

Ty turned to Brent, looking him up and down, a disgusted look on his face. "Stupid," he said.

They drove into the city of Worcester, ending up in a thin alley. At the end of the alley was an Escalade, like the one Brent had seen at his house a few days ago. His vision was getting cloudy and he struggled to keep awake. Ty stopped behind the Escalade and got out of the car. Brent tried to move his hand to unlock the seatbelt. He tried to gather his wits and will to tear the seatbelt out of its buckle if necessary, but he couldn't do either. A man came up to Brent's side of the car, a dark-skinned man with curly hair and a black beard. *Afghan,* thought Brent fleetingly.

"I think I gave him too much," said Ty, as the man leaned on the roof to peer into the open window. Brent forced himself to make note of the man, the scar across the forehead and eye, his black eyes, the shape of his face. *Need to remember. Need to tell the captain.*

"He is out. It is enough." The man whistled sharply, and more men came out of the Escalade. The dark haired man opened the door, reached over to unbuckle the seatbelt. Brent was unable to stop him. He tried to move away, but two men roughly grabbed him and hauled him out of the seat. He tried to kick, but he couldn't move his legs, and was dragged to the Escalade. Someone threw a sack over his head and tossed him into the SUV. He tried to stay conscious for the ride, but they all spoke Arabic and the ride was smooth. His head lolled to the side and he fell asleep.

FOURTEEN

He vaguely felt someone pull him out of the car. He threw up the beer, his mother's dinner, probably even breakfast. They pulled him by his shoulders, his toes dragging on the ground. He opened his eyes to see the bright night. The moon was to his left. He tried to orient himself, but had no idea where he was. He didn't know if he was even still in Worcester.

Brent tried to pull himself away, but someone yanked his arms back behind him. One yelled at another. They weren't speaking Pashtun, the language of Afghanistan that he was semi-familiar with. He felt a burst against his head and he was sent blissfully back into nothingness.

He could feel his consciousness returning again. It felt hot. Stifling. No air moved. His hands were numb. He breathed in, and it hurt. His toes were on something solid. He opened his eyes to see nothing but a dark room. He realized his arms were above his head, tied together at the wrist. He hung by his wrists, his toes barely touching a desk or chair below him. He moved his body side to side to see if he could wiggle out of it, but all he realized was that his wrists were looped around something metallic that clanked as he moved. He stood on tiptoes to see if he could unloop his wrists, but he scraped his thumb on a piece of sharp metal. He looked up, trying to see in the blackness what held him there. He couldn't tell what it was.

He looked around the room, seeing darker shapes against the darkness. A counter, embedded in the wall to his left, registered as slightly grey in the dark. When he looked down he saw he was on a chair, because he could see the back of it in the dark. His legs were taped together at the ankles. He was still in his clothes from the party, though he smelled horrible, the vomit drying on his shirt.

Can you fly, Magic Man?

Of course, I can fly.

He thought the spell, and set it loose. Nothing happened for a moment.

My spell didn't work? But they always work—

Then, suddenly, he felt a punch in the stomach, up into his ribs. He cried out as he exhaled most of the air out of his lungs. His body bent forward, his feet falling from the chair. In a panic, he tried to scramble with his bare feet back onto the chair, but instead succeeded in kicking it over. He cried out again when he fell down, feeling his shoulder almost give way.

"What the fuck was that?" he asked the empty room.

He twisted in the hot room. Then the lights burst on like firecrackers set off right in front of him. He closed his eyes, wincing. He heard the scraping of something at a door, and he tried to swing himself to turn around to face the sound. He couldn't quite do it, but someone grabbed him and did it for him.

The man from the Escalade stood in the doorway, dressed in dark-colored Afghan men's clothes, the loose-fitting tunic and pants. A scar crossed his face near his eye, and pock marks were on both cheeks. Two men stood next to Brent, dressed in black, wearing knives in a bandoleer style across their chest. Brent looked from one to the other, then back at the one he chose to call Scar.

He began the litany that he was taught when he would be caught by an enemy combatant. "Master Sergeant Brent Rogers—"

Thug 1 punched him in the face. He had a thicker, bushier beard than Thug 2, which was how Brent could tell them apart.

"You will not speak unless I speak to you, Sergeant," said Scar in impeccable English. "I will ask the questions, and you will answer."

Brent said nothing. He would conserve his power and anger for the right time.

"Tell me about the dragons."

Brent knew he looked confused for a moment. "The what?"

Thug 2 slammed a fist into his stomach. It hurt as much as the blow earlier.

"I said I will ask the questions."

"That wasn't a question."

Thug 1 slapped him. Scar snapped something at the two men. They stepped back, but still within arm's length of Brent.

"What do you know about the dragons?"

"I don't know anything about any dragons."

"You're a magician, are you not? A sorcerer? A witch?"

"I don't know what you're talking about." *Deny the Magic Corps to any enemy,* he had been told since the first day in Magic Corps training.

Scar walked over, a small smile on his face. "Sergeant Rogers. We are the Black Lions, and we know what you are. You have told enough people."

Black Lions? Who are they?

"You told your friends, your family. They all know, and they told others. Like your friend Muhammad."

"I don't have a friend Muhammad."

"Ah, yes. You called him by his old name, Tybalt."

Traitor, he thought, as the fury came up to his throat. He could feel the magic in him, screaming to get out. *Not yet.*

"You will tell me of the dragons."

"I don't know anything about any dragons."

"You will have to suffer broken bones and flesh, Sergeant. I was hoping to avoid that."

I can heal myself, he thought. Both men grabbed him by the waist and yanked him down.

He heard the pop as his right shoulder came out of its socket, and he screamed at the white-hot pain that came with it. He howled in agony as they dug their fingers into his shoulder, until Scar issued a sharp command. Brent whimpered as Scar took Brent's chin. "Dragons."

"I don't know--I swear to God."

"A shame." Scar released him. "How are you trained?"

Now would be a good time to hit him. Brent gathered up his will and threw it outward, meaning to slam all three men at the same time. Again, nothing happened. Again, he got hit, but this time twice as hard. Again, he swung backward as he got hit in the gut, seemingly straight through to his spine.

Scar grinned at him. "Your magic does not work here."

Brent could see that.

166

"Who trained you?"

Brent said nothing. He was kicked, punched, slapped. A question, no answer, a hit.

He knew he had broken bones. He spat out blood. His left eye closed from a series of punches in the head. His right shoulder burned in pain.

He had said nothing.

Scar jerked his head toward the area behind Brent. The two men, their knuckles bloody and swollen, walked away. Scar followed them, not saying another word. The lights flicked off.

He was left hanging in the dark. He had said nothing. He didn't tell them anything.

How long could he survive? He tried to use a little magic for healing the gash, but he got hit again, the time at the same place as the wound. He couldn't even use magic to heal himself. He hung his head, which hurt more.

He tried to sleep, but the pain was too much. He was thirsty, hungry, in that order.

He must've passed out, because the lights flashed on and he jerked his head up, snapping open his eyes. A boy, who looked about ten or twelve, came in with a bottle of Gatorade and a straw. He came up to Brent's groin. He stood there and held the Gatorade up. Brent struggled to get at the straw. The boy moved it so he could grab it with his lips. He sucked greedily. It was like the nectar of the gods. Then he realized he wouldn't be able to go anywhere to take a piss.

The boy took the bottle away and ran off. He slammed shut the door but left the lights on. Brent took that moment to look around with his one open eye. There were counters all around, and the room wasn't very big. He looked up to see that he was hanging by a hook with handcuffs. It was hot, the air still. He sweat into the open wounds, the salt burning them. He was in a secured room, like a freezer, but it wasn't on. A little while later, the lights turned off.

A long time after that, when his bladder was full, the lights came back on and Scar entered, this time with two other men, both in masks. Head to toe in black, they carried batons.

"Tell me about the dragons."

"I don't know anything—"

Crack, in his right injured shoulder. He screamed without meaning to. They assaulted him from behind, as the questions kept coming. He never knew where they would hit him. Then he felt something stab into his left shoulder and dig. The pain was agonizing, he felt his flesh tear away from his back. Something hooked into his left shoulder, and pulled on the bone.

He broke. He told them about the training from day one. Who trained him. Named names, even while they continued to dig the hook in his shoulder.

"Very good," said Scar finally. "Now, about the dragons."

"I DON'T KNOW ABOUT DRAGONS!"

Scar waved a hand. The two men stepped away. Brent had pissed his pants, his head was hung down in shame. One man raised his mask and spit on him. Scar turned and walked out, the two men following.

The lights went out. Brent let the tears fall.

He didn't know how long it was, but he had passed out again. He heard scratching behind him. He tried to turn around. He thought he heard a gunshot against the door. He could have sworn it was there. Then he heard it again. The door swung open.

Distilled light flowed into the room. A large black wolf came in, followed by two grey wolves. His heart leapt, knowing who the black wolf was. "Tony," he said, his voice like gravel.

A man's large shadow filled the door frame, and he came into the room. "It *is* you," the man said.

"Reese?" Brent whispered. "What're you doing here?" He looked at Tony, then Reese.

"Time for stories later. Let's get you out of here."

One of the greys huffed, and sat down. The big black wolf snapped at him. The grey got up.

Reese took out a knife and cut the duct tape that bound his feet. He lifted Brent and unhooked him from above. Brent fell forward, his shoulder slamming into Reese's back, as he groaned in pain. "Did a number on you," said Reese, carrying him over his shoulder out of the room.

As they turned the corner, Reese came to a stop. "Shit," he hissed, and dove back around the corner. He set Brent down on the floor. With seemingly no effort, Reese twisted the link between the handcuff and separated his two wrists. The pain in his shoulders made him swallow a cry as his arms came to rest at his sides.

Reese handed Brent a pistol. He waved it at Brent, a questioning look on his face. Brent ignored his pain and reached for the pistol. He could barely squeeze his swollen index finger through the trigger guard.

Reese held up four fingers, and pointed left. Brent nodded. *There are four men on the left hand side.* Reese looked at the two wolves. He pointed left. *You go left.* They seemed to nod. Brent noticed he was in an unused kitchen, and before him was a door that swung into the kitchen and outward to the main room.

Reese shouldered his AK-47 and stood up. He burst through the swinging door hugging the right, firing as he moved. The wolves dove left, and the door swung shut.

"Shit!" yelled Reese. Brent didn't know if that was a good "shit" or a bad "shit."

Brent sat there, awkwardly aiming the pistol at the door from his hip to shoot whoever or whatever came in. He heard more shooting. "On your six, Tony!" yelled Reese suddenly, and a burst of fire erupted through the kitchen door, making Brent dive to the floor, sending white-hot pain through his back and arms.

An Afghan burst through the kitchen door. Brent raised the gun up with his wrists, still shooting from his hip, but something tackled the Afghan from behind, one of the gray wolves. It attached itself to the back of the man's neck, as he was screaming. He rolled, trying to get the wolf off of him. Brent didn't have a clear shot, and even if he did, Brent didn't think he could get him.

Brent followed the man's head with his gun, and the wolf jumped up, tearing flesh away from the man's neck. The man was facing Brent. Brent held the gun from his waist and fired.

The man fell backward, the back of his head splattered on the bottom of the stainless steel oven door.

Reese swung the door open as Brent turned with the gun, aiming it at him. Reese held up his hands, the AK hanging from a strap across his chest. "Some got away," he said. He bent down and picked Brent up, setting him on his feet, then hoisting him over his shoulder again. Brent dropped the gun. Reese bent and picked it up, saying, "C'mon, let's get outta here."

FIFTEEN

"You okay?" Lori stood at the side of the bed, studying him. She wore her scrubs, having either come from work or her lunch hour.

Brent forced a smile. "I'm okay," he said. His mother was sitting on the only chair next to the bed. She didn't move out of the way for Lori to get closer.

Finally, after the silence stretched so long as to be uncomfortable, she said, "I can't stay. I'll come back as soon as I can." She gave him a kiss on the cheek and walked out of the room. He watched her go, stuffing a sigh of relief. He really wanted to sleep, not to entertain guests. That included his mother.

"Mom," said Brent turning to her. "Go home. I'm okay here."

"Don't be mad at your father."

"Why should I be mad at him?" He knew that his father, for obvious reasons, wouldn't be allowed on the case. However, Tony was.

"You're just so quiet."

"I hurt, Mom."

She jumped up. "I can get the doctor—"

"Mom, please? Please. Just…" *Just leave me alone.* She had been with him from the moment he woke up, and hadn't left. He wanted some privacy. Some time to rest.

He didn't mean to, but she looked dejected anyway. "Okay, honey. Okay. I'll be back tomorrow."

He kissed her cheek when she bent over to kiss him. "Thanks."

As soon as she cleared the doorway, he turned off the light. He turned over, as best as he could with his sore shoulders, and thought he heard, "I think he's sleeping."

"Tony?" He reached up, and turned the light back on. Brent sat up in bed as Tony came in, Luke following him.

Tony looked roughed up in his suit. He asked, "How are you?"

"Sore, beat up, but they gave me morphine."

"I saw your mom."

"I hope she's not mad."

"She's a cop's wife," said Tony. "She'll get it." Tony didn't move to sit down.

Luke walked to the foot of the bed. "Tomorrow we will have to ask you questions."

Tony nodded. "Today, we're visiting."

Brent smiled. "Thanks. How did you find me?"

Tony looked at Luke. "Luke found an abandoned restaurant that had its electricity turned on two days ago."

"We guessed," said Luke. "We also talked to the owner of the building."

"The owner is in Saudi Arabia and didn't authorize having the electricity turned on."

"How do you know Reese?"

Tony ran his hand through his own hair. "I owed some vamps a favor." He glanced at Luke, who betrayed nothing.

"Bates?" asked Brent.

"He's the big man in this town," said Tony. "Nothing happens under the moonlight that he doesn't know."

Luke said, "The man you call Reese is a federal agent. Of course, when the FBI is involved, the precinct must comply."

"I thought the boss was going to have kittens when the FBI said it was a terrorist kidnapping."

"Black Lions," said Brent. "They called themselves Black Lions." He brushed at his blanket, not meeting their eyes. "They know a lot now. The pain was…"

"Brent," said Luke kindly. Brent didn't look up at him. "Brent. You were afraid for your life."

Brent shrugged and winced, his shoulder flaring in pain. They weren't going to reset his shoulder until the swelling had gone down. He knew from asking people that he was gone for three days, was malnourished, had stitches in his forehead, broken ribs, torn out bits of flesh from his shoulders, a concussion—the list was nearly endless.

"Sorry," said Tony. "We'd better go, let you get some rest."

"Thanks. Thanks for finding me."

"We'll be back." Luke smiled, patted his bed, and left the room. Tony nodded and winked, heading out as well.

A nurse came in. "Do you think I could get something for sleep?"

"Of course," she said. However, when she returned two hours later with something for him, he was already passed out from exhaustion.

⭐   ⭐   ⭐

Brent woke up to see the window beside him shattered. A male nurse came into the room while he studied it. "Morning," said the nurse. "Do you remember anything about last night?"

He shook his head.

"You somehow threw one of our nurses into the window."

Brent looked down, embarrassed. "I'm sorry. I didn't mean to. I know magic," Brent said, as the nurse came around with the blood pressure machine.

"Excuse me?"

"Magic. I'm in the Army. I must have used a spell."

The nurse put the blood pressure cuff on him. "Magic, eh?"

"It's not commonly discussed."

"I never heard of magic like that, to be honest. But I'll take your word for it." He wrote down the numbers from the machine, took Brent's temperature. "Any pain?"

"Yes."

"Do you need another morphine? You don't want to chase the pain, you want to keep it at bay."

"What's the usual dosage? I don't want to be an addict."

"We can switch to something not as strong, how's that?"

"That sounds good."

"I'll ask the doctor." The nurse looked at the window. "Maintenance will be in to board up the window."

However, his breakfast arrived. Brent's stomach rumbled. The nurse said, "You should regain your strength. No more magic for you."

"Doctor's orders?" asked Brent, looking at the tray expectantly.

"They can be."

Brent smiled and slowly lifted the cover from his tray. He saw eggs, a muffin, and butter, bacon, and coffee. He looked at the fork, and thought it was going to take a large degree of effort to eat.

"Good morning, Sergeant."

Brent looked up to see a man in a long purple robe in the doorway. Brent sat up straighter and tried to salute.

"At ease," said the man, coming into the room. "How do you feel?"

"Like crap, Master Pike."

Pike had a patch of a wand with stars over his breast pocket, a member of the magic corps. He had stars on his collar. Brent knew him; he had trained Brent in healing. Pike passed a hand over Brent. "You're needed."

"Yes, sir."

"If you were healed, think you could come back immediately?"

"Yes, sir."

Another man in a lab coat came in. "Excuse me," he said, looking at Pike. "Who are you?"

"I'm a healer," he said, holding out his hand. "Colonel Noel Pike."

"Doctor Thomas Tetrault. A healer?"

"Yes. Magic."

"I'm sorry?"

Brent looked helplessly at the ceiling. "Just believe me," said Pike. "I'm here to examine our young man and heal him if necessary."

"Magic is no substitute for natural healing."

"Tell me, doctor, how much magic have you seen?"

The doctor didn't look at him. "I don't agree with this. Not at all."

"Doctor, I don't particularly care if you agree or not. I will heal him, sign him out, and he will report directly to duty."

The doctor shook his head.

Pike turned away from the doctor, looked at Brent. "Are you ready for duty?"

"Yes, sir," said Brent, trying to sit up straighter.

The doctor was already heading out the door, presumably to get security. Pike said to Brent, "Relax. This won't hurt."

Brent closed his eyes. He felt the warm, healing energy wash over him like a calm lake wave against a shore, easing his pain. He sighed as the red-hot aura of agony eased, his shoulders stopped throbbing. He felt suspended in water, cocooned in comfortable a warm lake.

Then it faded, and both men opened their eyes in unison. "Better?"

Brent rolled his right shoulder. No clicking, no pain. He took a deep breath. It didn't hurt. "Good as new."

"I'll let the doctor know you're ready to go."

"Let me call some people, tell them I'm leaving."

"Call them while I look for the doctor."

Brent tried to call his mother, but there was no answer. He didn't get his father or Tony. He tried Chrissie. She picked up on the third ring. "Hi, Chrissie."

"Brent! Are you okay? I heard —"

"Chrissie, listen. The Army's picking me up right now. Can I write you?"

"Of course. Of course you can. Send me pictures, too. I'll write you—what's your address?"

He gave her his address as the doctor walked in. He waited, Pike behind him. "I have to go, hon," he said, the term of endearment slipping out. "I'll call you again as soon as I can."

"Be safe, Magic Man."

"I will, promise." He hung up. The doctor came forward. "Let me see your shoulder." The doctor examined it, moved it, then leaned back. "I'm going to do some x-rays."

"We don't have time for that," said Pike. "We'll do the x-rays in Kabul."

Brent wasn't sure why he was happy to be going back to Afghanistan. The only one who might understand would be his father or Tony. His mother wouldn't.

He tried his dad again and this time got through. "Dad, the Army's here to take me."

"Already?"

"I guess they need me."

His father muttered, "I guess. Did you tell your mother?"

"She's not answering. The office said she's not there, either."

"When are you leaving?"

He looked up to see Pike walking out of the room again. "Soon, I think."

"That could mean minutes or hours. Keep trying to get your mother. Leave a note if you have to." He paused for a minute, and said, "Be careful. Call me when you can. Good luck."

"Thanks, Dad."

The morning nurse came back in, Colonel Pike stood in the doorway. "Here's your discharge papers. Do you have any clothes?"

"Uh…no."

Said Pike, "He will." He motioned to Brent and got out of the doorway. "Get off the bed."

Brent did, wearing only a johnny. Pike straightened out the blanket. "What's your size?"

"Large, 32-34."

Pike took out a small plastic bag. He tore off the corner and sprinkled red sand into a rough circle, then sprinkled symbols inside it. He raised his hands in benediction, chanting. Brent knew it was a summoning, though he didn't know what he was summoning. Then, there was a pop, and a stench of burned eggs. In the circle was a pair of folded jeans and a folded t-shirt, tags still on them.

"I'll apologize to the Milwaukee Wal-Mart later," said Pike.

Said Brent, "You're originally from Milwaukee?" He knew that a person could summon articles from a place that he already knew.

"Born and bred," said Pike. "Get dressed."

Brent lifted the clothes, the stink still on them, and underneath was a pair of sneakers. He pulled on the clothes. The sneakers were a little big, but better than too small.

He was tying his sneakers when his mother came in. She looked worried. "They said you were discharged." She glanced at Pike. "Hello."

"Ma'am," he said, inclining his head. "We need to take your son in for a debriefing."

"Now? But his shoulder—"

"Healed, Mom." Brent had hoped to avoid this. He wanted to leave without the overly tearful farewell he had gotten at Logan Airport when he left for Boot.

His mother raised her head. He thought she would be defiant. "Oh," she said, and looked at Pike. "I guess you did that?"

"Yes, ma'am."

Brent thought hard. *Please don't cry. I don't want to leave you like that.*

"Well," she said. "I'd better not keep the Army waiting." She put down her purse and hugged him fiercely. "Be careful. Write. Call."

"Yes, Mom."

She looked at Pike. "Take care of him."

"We will, ma'am."
Brent left the room, not looking back. He was going home.

www.ingramcontent.com/pod-product-compliance
Lightning Source LLC
Chambersburg PA
CBHW050941120626
46552CB00001B/318